THE LOST MEMORIES
OF
OCEANS

THE LOST MEMORIES OF OCEANS

R. TIM MORRIS

ISBN: 979-8-8878500-3-0 (Paperback)
ISBN: 979-8-8878500-4-7 (Hardcover)
-
Library of Congress Control Number: 2022945175

Any references to historical events, real people, or real places are used fictitiously. Names, characters, and places are products of the author's imagination.

Branch image by brgfx via Freepik.
Book design by Allison Chernutan.

Printed in the United States of America.

First printing edition 2022.

emily@fracturedmirrorpublishing.com
Fractured Mirror Publishing
Knoxville, Tennessee

www.fracturedmirrorpublishing.com

TO ANY READER WHO HAS EVER FALLEN
INTO AN INCREDIBLE NEW WORLD

PORTEOUS

ERW
["ROO"]

THE HIDDEN ISLAND
THE HOUSE IN THE WOODS
KOLE'S VILLAGE

THE SCARRED YARDS
YARARI
 NT SHRINE
WOODS
BLUEBELL FIELD
THE FAERIE HILLS
THISTLEMOOR
THE SATYR WOODS
WOODLAND RIVER
THE FOREST of REDD
TOWER MOUNTAIN
SIER WOODS
THE SPINE OF THE WORLD
SCEANTH
["SANTH"]

CHAPTER
1

THE SATYR NARROWED HIS HORRIBLE BRONZE EYES. "WHY DO you not fear things, Nettle?"

"I am not without fear," she spat at him defensively. "Far from it, Brawn."

"So prove it, then." Brawn remained reclined upon his monstrous throne, carved from a massive branch, blackened from the fire that burned his once-favorite tree to nearly nothing. Now the throne resided inside his woodland den, a comfort for him when his own troubles and the frailties of others weighed heavily on his mind. Like in this moment. His jittery legs gave away a thin facade of fortitude, however; his hooves rattled nervously upon the branch. "Prove it to me."

Their breaths were thick in the cold, as the world outside the satyr's den—the land of Sceanth—had been blanketed by snow a half-moon ago. The icy temperatures affected Nettle very little; she was a bluebell faerie after all, and as such, she was not bothered by frivolities like the changing weather. Brawn disliked the cold, preferring to remain in his home over trekking outside.

He drank to warm himself, guzzling a foul-smelling drink from a worn goblet that was never far from his reach.

Nettle disliked the constant presence of his goblet, and oftentimes imagined herself crushing it with a river stone. She said, "I cannot disprove an absence of fear! You ask the impossible of me."

"You let yourself into *my* home, like all the many times before. Yet, *this* time you tell me it is the end of us? Like it's just so simple! What about regrets? Emotional consequences? A fear of what comes next? You know none of that, Nettle. Not like *I* do." His horns were still little more than nubs, having been late to start growing. "Prove it to me," he said again, leaning closer to the faerie. "Tell me what it is you fear, Nettle."

She shrunk into herself while choosing her answer carefully. "I am afraid of loving someone unintentionally," Nettle said. "And not knowing if there might be someone else I should be loving more."

Brawn blinked slowly, trying to comprehend. He'd never heard such thoughts from the faerie. "Bluebells love *everything*, do they not? Here and there, and all at once?"

"I…my love is…it is *different*." With a sharp finger, Nettle scratched at a burl upon the inside of the den; the knobby, malformed growth had a sinister shape to it. The amber-pink glow which surrounded her began to dim a little. "Somehow, it is tied to an ocean I cannot see. My love is incomplete. I fear it always will be."

"The ocean?" Brawn huffed a little at the faerie's pining for something she would never find. "And yet, you know for certain that you and I…That we—?"

"What I *know* is…I just know we are *wrong*, Brawn. If our tryst were meant to remain a secret, it was likely never meant to have been at all." Nettle picked at some winter pollen that had become stuck to her wing. She released it from her fingertip, and the mote floated away, finding its own path out of the den. "And maybe I'm wrong about what it is I fear, but I'm not going to fear my decision to leave. That is all I can say."

Nettle followed the bit of pollen out into the woods, hoping that, with a change of scenery, they might both find some form of happiness elsewhere. She wiped the tears from her eyes quickly, wishing she would soon forget her many mistakes. Brawn did not leave his den. He did not call after her; the satyr was already too lost in thoughts of his next drink to say anything more.

Fleeing Brawn's home for what she hoped would be the last time, Nettle flew directly to the bluebell fields. There was a light, misty haze over everything, but through the haze and around snowy hilltops, one could find the faerie enchantment field, a sparkling dome of magick which not only kept the winter out, but also kept the bluebells bright all year. Nettle's mother, Cleo, was sitting on a large rock just inside the faerie enchantment. Her large, luminescent wings fanned the air around her; a few voros moths playfully dipped and dove around the breeze. A sparkling blue stream splashed by her feet, flowing out beyond the enchantment field where the gentle current began to freeze.

Without wasting a moment, Cleo spoke, for she knew when her daughter carried troubles with her. "You are shaken, Nettle. What thoughts have you brought with you?"

Nettle crouched within some bluebells and allowed a few of the flowers to tickle her palms. "I bring nothing, Mother."

Cleo smiled quickly, dismissively. "We all carry something that cannot be seen." She breathed in slowly, trying to absorb the scent of each and every petal surrounding her. Nothing was quite as comforting as her bluebell fields. She watched as her daughter attempted to leave thoughts behind in the flowers, to try to forget something weighing on her mind. All too obvious for a mother to not notice. "The patterns have shifted, daughter."

"Which patterns?"

"Of the bluebells. Sometimes they grow from the ground in specific ways, telling their stories—writing them upon the great lands of Sceanth. If a magick is strong enough, it can influence how the flowers will grow. But only from above will you see their patterns."

Nettle observed the field around her, sensing nothing special. "And what is the pattern I find myself in now, Mother?"

Cleo responded with a wink. "I cannot say from down here." A strange chirping noise came from the voros moths. Nettle had not heard them make such a sound before. Cleo looked out beyond the enchantment field, toward the snow-capped forests. "You've been away for a time."

"That I have, Mother."

"Far be it from me to ask where." Cleo's toes stretched and made circles beneath the stream, like tiny creatures with minds of their own. "Or with *whom*."

Tentatively, Nettle asked, "Have you spoken with Piper, Mother?"

"*Your* Piper?"

"Yes." Nettle's eyes darted around, but no one else seemed to be nearby. "My Piper, yes." Though Nettle kept her encounters with Brawn hidden from all, her relationship with the whimsical, beautiful bluebell Piper was no secret.

Cleo stood tall atop the large rock and folded her wings beneath her skin in a smooth, elegant motion. The moths fluttered away, uninterested in the impending discussion. "Nettle. I'm speaking not about whom you choose to love, nor about those whose love you might find comfort in."

"What *are* you saying, Mother?"

"Are you not happy here, Daughter?"

"Mostly. I suppose. It's just that—"

"Do you not love? Are you not loved in return?"

Immediately, Nettle recalled her earlier discussion with Brawn. "I am, Mother. Though I cannot help but wonder what love might be elsewhere. If only the ocean—"

"Again with thoughts of the ocean. We are not meant for the ocean, Nettle. Nothing good will come of it."

"I will save it for my dreams then, Mother," she said, turning back down to the flowers.

Cleo knew her daughter would answer with those very words. "There are dangers, Nettle. Dangers that other worlds bring."

Nettle's hands fell into her lap. "Dangers?"

"Hmmm. Of entering other worlds, and of becoming a part of those worlds. It is a darkness that, if in too deep, bluebell fae may not find their way out of."

Somewhere, Nettle thought—beyond the bluebells, the frozen stream, the icy groves, and through the frosted woods—a satyr laughed vengefully.

Cleo stood from the river and fluttered closer to her daughter. "Choose your life veins carefully, Daughter. Choose them wisely. And they, in turn, will choose the right path for you." She held out a hand, nearly placing it upon Nettle's shoulder. "Let your fears guide your choices."

Nettle could only stare unblinkingly at her mother and the ways she could proclaim such life lessons. And she still did not know whether her mother knew of Nettle's tryst with the satyr, or if she spoke of future trials. "I've been told I do not fear things."

"And who has told you this? Piper?"

Nettle bit her tongue. "No. It was not Piper."

Cleo studied her daughter closely, but seemingly her gaze could not pierce Nettle's secrets. Finally, she said, "You have much of your father in you."

Nettle tried to remember the happy moments with her father, but more often than not, she found herself remembering mostly nothing. She did recall him talking at great lengths about an ocean. She tugged at a bluebell stem, almost pulling it from the ground.

"He was always searching for something. Always on the go. Wanderlust. He should have known he'd only end up more lost after gifting that human."

"I will choose to give my gifts more carefully."

There was a sense that her mother did not wish for Nettle to share gifts at all. She paused before selecting a more diplomatic answer. "If you choose a human, you have not been careful enough. Just like your father." Cleo flapped her hand, motioning for Nettle to stand. "You will know when the time is right, Daughter. But for your sake, I hope that time does not find you."

"But why, Mother?"

"Gifting another bears much responsibility. And the consequences can sometimes be unfair."

"Unfair?"

Cleo chose to keep any further thoughts to herself. "I only hope the best for you." Then she placed her palms on her daughter's shoulders. "Your cocoon. You've had your time with it, bluebell daughter. But your dreams will only worsen. You must dissolve it—*destroy* it—before it destroys *you*." She leaned closer and breathed words into her daughter's ear. "Have you chosen your life veins carefully, Nettle?"

Both her mother's warnings and the echoes of Brawn's petulance found their way back into Nettle's head. Over and over she heard them. But the presence of the voros moths hovering alongside her eased her mind, and she glided through the woods undeterred. On thin, glimmering wings, she fluttered past familiar trees, farther and farther away from the bluebell fields until golden sunbeams failed to pierce through the forest's canopy.

She was headed for her cocoon. Her life vein cocoon, the location of which she had kept hidden on the outskirts of the satyrs' woods. Once inside, and against her mother's wishes, she would dream again; and although she could never predict which dreams she might have, she invariably hoped to see the ocean.

The ocean mattered to her.

Nothing else in the land of Sceanth mattered. None of it. Her mother, her wayward father, Piper, Brawn and his horrible, stinking goblet. Even the wonderful voros moths. Nettle would give it all up to find the ocean, and the love it kept for her, folded within its waves.

Hidden behind a mossy log and beneath some large, browning ferns hung her cocoon. The perfect, wood-like sphere was still intact, just as she'd left it. Nettle breathed a sigh of relief having worried the satyr might have harmed it in revenge.

The shell had a careful, purposeful crack in it. With both hands, Nettle pulled the shell away; the opening was just large enough for her small frame to enter. Careful to not catch her ivory dress on the edge, she then kissed the voros moths good-bye before entering her life vein cocoon. Hopefully, she thought, for what might be the last time. Though there was a part of her that stopped momentarily to smile at the idea of returning once more, if only to misappropriate Brawn's favored goblet.

Then she slipped inside to dream again.

CHAPTER
2

When bluebell faeries dream in their life vein cocoons, many choose the first life veins they find. Other fae are far more careful and take their time making the right choice.

Nettle found it difficult to make any choice at all in her cocoon. Mostly, she was unsure how to choose the right one.

In the moments before she woke up in a different world, Nettle dreamed many terrible things. She dreamed of the broken bones of the dead falling from the sky. Undecipherable bits of creatures, pitter pattering upon mole hills of wet soil. The river haunted her too; eyes of murky red glowered from deep beneath, watching her as she scuttled along the water's surface. A thick mist crept in, at first nothing more than wet dew on her sharp cheeks, but before long concealing everything in sight. The air smelled of brackish mud and centuries-old plant life. Then rot and decay.

And then, finally, a scream. A woman's flesh-rending scream.

Nettle woke in a darkness grayed by the moonlight. Her faint, amber-pink glow did little to illuminate her surroundings.

Oddly, she was not occupying any of the usual spaces she typically found herself in upon waking. Instead, she was in a bed, in a bedroom, presumably within a house. When Nettle was not dreaming in her life vein cocoon, she would sleep in beds of leaves, or maybe balled up on a high, curled tree branch just outside the faerie enchantment field. Even a wet, rocky cave would do. Here, the wooden floorboards seemed to creak on their own. A couple of windowpanes rattled slightly, and the winds tickled already-weathered glass. Through the thin walls she could hear the soft fizz of rain upon tall grass and reeds. The distant ocean was in her head, too. Nettle was certain she could place the sound of crashing waves on remote rocks, the timed lapping upon the shoreline, and the tang of salt and the stink of kelp.

The ocean.

It was lovely in its uncertainty.

However, her thoughts and memories immediately went to dark places. To the day before, when she spoke with Brawn. Her wings hurt as she recalled his words, her tears, and the heaviness of hearts as she glided away from his woodland den one last time. The last talk with her mother, Cleo, who warned Nettle about the dangers of dreams of other worlds—the ocean especially—going so far as to suggest her daughter finally dissolve her life vein cocoon.

And now this strange house. Nettle wondered, if only for a moment, whether Brawn was playing a spiteful trick on her. But the satyr had only recently begun dabbling in magicks of his own; he was nowhere near the level of skill required for such deception.

On glimmering wings, Nettle fluttered a couple of feet to the window. She wiped the thin layer of dust and dirt from the glass with the sleeve of her ivory white dress. The fog on the other side proved just as bothersome as the dirt, concealing whatever existed beyond her immediate surroundings.

Turning, she floated out of the room. Down the black hallway, Nettle spotted a thin light downstairs. This place was strange, she thought. Rooms like these did not exist on Sceanth, certainly nowhere near the bluebell fields she was used to. As she descended, even flying, the stair joints creaked as though her bare feet touched the steps. But maybe it was nothing more than a ghost, shadowing her every move through the house? Normally, thoughts like that would never send a chill up her spine, but Nettle shivered a little at the idea.

It was an expansive foyer at the bottom of the stairs. Sour-smelling crimson curtains hung heavily over the windows. Hand-drawn nautical maps and some empty picture frames adorned the yellowed walls, all tilted at curious, crooked angles. There was a pair of charcoal drawings: one of an island and the other of a tiny black boat. Ocean waves besieged each of the subjects. Skillful drawings, both of them. A lengthy, mildewed carpet ran from the staircase to the front door, which had been left slightly ajar. Whether this was a sign of neglect from some-one leaving or entering, Nettle could not know. The old, heavy wood was moist and mossy. The faerie again used her dirtied sleeve to open it enough to flutter outside, ever closer to the rumbling waters.

The fog was thick, but the old house appeared to be in the middle of a densely wooded marshland. In the far distance were the sounds of ocean waves pummeling the shore. A trail lined with tall grass and brush led from the house to a mass of spotted and peeling birch trees. Rain sprinkled through the fog, but Nettle did not mind the misty wetness. Just as in Sceanth, and despite wearing only a thin dress, the cold did not bother her.

Nettle also did not mind planting her feet on the ground. The bits of pebbles and bent twigs littered across wet soil felt wonderful beneath her naked soles. Though she was gifted with butterfly-like, iridescent wings, Nettle still enjoyed the sensa-tion of such an anchored connection to her world. Or in dream worlds. Or even *this* world. But she kept her wings unfolded, just in case she suddenly needed to fly.

Stepping along the trail, Nettle came to some berry bushes. Only a smattering of rotted berries remained on the branches, black and red ones of different varieties. Mostly, the ground served as a muddy graveyard for decayed fruits. She reached past thorny canes to pluck a wilted blackberry, and it shriveled to nearly nothing in her palm. Nettle tasted the graying, fuzzy layer with the tip of her ruby tongue. It was satisfying, and not unpleasant. She tasted the berry and asked questions of it. Through this connection, the decomposing berry spoke to Nettle: it said, "*Roo.*" Its language was slightly different than her own, but in her mind, Nettle visualized the word as "Erw," and knew instinctively that it was the same.

"Erw," she spoke aloud. And something inside her, some lingering dust of dreams past, told her this place was not unfamiliar. Nettle had seen it all before. "This land is called Erw." A thick brown slug turned its eyestalks toward her, telepathically confirming Nettle's discovery. "My name is Nettle. I have come to find your ocean," she spoke to it, though received nothing in return but some warbled sensory activity. She placed two fingertips along the length of the gastropod in an attempt to discern more information about this place. From what she could intuit, Erw was in no way as vast as her own lands of lush forests, colossal mountain ranges, bottomless valley canyons, and populated farmland clusters. Also, her real home was never so dreary or foreboding as this. Misty mornings were common in Nettle's world, but this fog was unrelenting. It had an undesirable way of scratching at one's insides and picking at one's thoughts. The déjà vu of dreams aside, Nettle knew she had never been inside a house such as the one she exited just minutes before; she'd spent her short lifetime in green forests and fields, and the more industrious creatures of Sceanth—mostly the humans— built their tiny homes from stone, never so uncivilized as to use tree wood for their dwellings. Erw's distant but ever-present ocean was abstruse, yet there remained an enthralling lure to it. A certain feeling—perhaps love? She hoped for such a thing, but couldn't put a finger on it.

Nettle removed her hand from the slug and dropped the remainder of the rotted berry, which it greedily began to consume, if it were possible for a slug to do anything at a greedy pace.

She turned back, but could no longer see the house; the fog had entirely enveloped its space in this world. Her feet remained on the path, and Nettle continued farther down the trail, the distant crashing waves of Erw's ocean calling her forth. There were eyes, either from one or a thousand creatures, within the trees watching her go on.

It just may have been the perfect moment to prove to Brawn the presence of fear within her.

<h1>CHAPTER
3</h1>

Nettle walked cautiously through the night along the path that led away from the old house in the woods. The tall birch trees had thinned, and marshlands became dewy fields; the trail still wound its way along, leading Nettle to somewhere unknown, unseen, and unavoidable. The sound of the ocean came and went, making it unclear whether the water was drawing nearer or whether she was heading somewhere else entirely. Her feet alternated between the intimate feeling of her toes on the earth and hovering inches above it. Finally, the trail became impassable, coming to an abrupt end at a hillside thicket. More berries had grown here, these ones of unknown, prickly varieties, and even more rotten than those found in the woods. Nettle dared not ask these berries what they might know. She fluttered above the thicket instead.

The fog was even more dense here—almost black—but she instinctively knew the ocean's maw lurked nearby. Soon enough, the thicket gave way to tall, brown grass, and Nettle buzzed along until coming to a hilltop, where she landed. The briny seaweed and saltwater stink blew up the hill from somewhere down below in the dark, misty nothingness. Cautiously, she stepped onward.

Monstrous, black things began to take form through the fog; boxy shapes of indefinite size. Perhaps they were giant monsters on the prowl, or possibly guardians of this watery destination. But the ominous shapes reformed the closer she came, and ultimately solidified into nothing more than a small, darkened fishing village. Nettle approached with trepidation.

There were many advantages to having beautiful, glowing faerie wings, but surely in this particular moment it was Nettle's ability to flutter closer to the dwellings in near silence. She dulled her wings' glow in order to explore without giving herself away. The first building she came upon was completely dark; only what little moonlight the fog had not absorbed had lit its façade. Peering through the window's mottled glass, Nettle's sharp eyesight could make out the incessantly creeping mist as it inched its way between rooms. Items were scattered everywhere, tools and boots and candles.

Again, she felt the persistent sense of being watched. Maybe it was the thick fog itself that had eyes on her?

Nettle wished to enter this place; she wanted to push up the window, to hear it rattle its way along old, worn wood. From outside, she could get a sense of the mildew and rotted, salty fish meat, but she wanted to smell it from even closer. Nettle found abandoned places to be oddly soothing; their idle, dead air was like a sanctuary to her. Not all faeries felt this way about these places, ones absent of life and breath, harbouring the forsaken pieces of the pasts of others.

She wished to enter, yet the fog seemed to wish her away.

The next dwelling over had a light outside. A lantern had been hung next to the front door, the oil wick alight. The flame flickered and its glow licked upon the gnarled, knotty surface of the wooden abode. Unless there were magicks involved, some creature must have lit this not so long ago. The door handle was cold and wet; it jiggled without effort, and Nettle slowly pushed the solid, weighty door open.

The creaking hinge sufficiently cloaked the frantic movement within.

Shadows jumped abruptly, and something hard hit Nettle in the jaw. She fell to her knees and looked up. There in front of her, brandishing an old, mud-crusted boot as a weapon, was a girl. "Who are you?" she asked Nettle, a certain amount of fear upon her face. "What brings you to my home, stranger?"

Nettle retracted her wings. The cramped quarters would not provide much space to fly, and if she were to be attacked again, the wings would only get in her way. "Do not hurt me! I—I am not of this world."

"Not of this world? All the more reason to strike you down!"

Nettle produced a pulsing, glimmering flare from her fingertips. Like bubbles, but they popped from existence almost as soon as they appeared. The effect was trance-inducing, and the girl wobbled backwards a little; she lowered her arms and dropped the muddy boot. It hit the floor with a heavy thud.

Nettle rubbed the pain from her jaw and hoped she had bought herself enough time to assess the situation. The girl was shaking her head, attempting to snap herself out of the hypnosis; but, before long, she gave in and slumped to the floor, too, holding onto a chair for support. "What…did you do to me?" she asked, trying her best to remain focused on the trespasser.

"I'm sorry," Nettle said. "Typically, my magicks are much more proficient at fending off intruders." Her palms and fingertips still glowed with residual energy, a faint lavender hue.

"It is *you* who is the intruder here, demon!"

Nettle ignored the girl and continued to consider the effects her enchantment had. "Either you are exceptionally powerful, which seems unlikely, or my magicks are weaker in this world." Nettle rose back to her feet and took in the details of the room while keeping the girl in her periphery.

This dwelling appeared less abandoned. She could tell not only by looking, but also through her other senses. There was the scent of candles, one still burning and others recently blown out. The home smelled of fish, but also of fully-stocked grains and preserves in the pantry. The distant echoes of recently walked-on floorboards were in the air. Despite it being lived in, the space was not well-tended; the floor had a dusty layer, candle wax had dried in drips and puddles nearly everywhere, and the walls were black and split like bark. There was a mantle above a cold iron hearth, and displayed upon it was a copper shrine of some sort that she touched softly with her fingertips, mostly to judge its density. The shrine's top came to a twisted point, almost snake-like in its form. A couple of weathered photographs were propped up on the mantle, too. Nettle recognized the girl who attacked her in one of them, along with a woman and a man. There were cracks of smiles upon their faces, like they were instructed to be serious but were perhaps thinking of something inappropriate instead. They posed in front of a low stone wall, tall grass and blowing beach sand frozen in time behind them.

Nettle turned back to the girl, who was still shaken and on the floor and staring at her indignantly. The fog had begun to slice its way through the open door and into the room, slightly muting both girls' presence. Her experience with the humans of Sceanth had been limited. Though humans and bluebell fae were of comparable sizes, that was mostly where their similarities ended, and Nettle was well aware of the parts of them she was meant to fear. She had a difficult time finding the words she wanted to say. "You—you look to be my age. How old are you?"

"Old enough to know not to slip into others' homes in the middle of the night." The girl began to rise now. Nettle stepped backwards, almost imperceptibly.

"My name is Nettle," she spoke in much the same tone as she had to the slug.

With an indistinct squint of the eyes, a clenched jaw, and gritted teeth, the girl hesitated for a moment. But she eventually barked, "Kole. I am Kole." Standing fully upright, Kole was nowhere as imposing as Nettle first believed. Neither attacking from the shadows nor brandishing a muddied boot went a long way, too. Kole had short, mussed hair and a strong, shovel-like jawline. Her eyes were a tone slightly grayer than black. A green tattoo of some sort—something like a bolt of lightning or a creeping vine—peeked out from a high-necked fishing sweater, running up to her earlobe. All her clothes were brown, though it may have been the fog obscuring the dim lighting in the room. She rubbed one eye with a palm to remove the last of the flare's effects. "Tell me, are you really from another world?"

"That might depend on whether you believe in other worlds."

Kole crossed her arms, but then brought them back to her sides, as though not yet ready to let her guard down. "There are many frightening things that exist here in Erw. The ocean, for one. The howling of our trees. A sense of always being watched…

"I have felt it, yes."

"Darkness takes many forms that remain unseen. Creatures big and small, full of malevolent tricks and brimming with chaos. But their existence mostly remain in the form of hushed rumors and tales of warning. Your presence, however—"

It was clear Kole believed in many things she had never once seen. Yet, here stood Nettle: her eyes a glassy and iridescent blue-green; her skin the color of almond; chin and cheekbones sharp as though freshly chiseled from slate; fingers long, thin, and somewhat exaggerated in their needle-like points. The unremitting presence of monsters and unspeakable horrors in Erw was unseen but wholly accepted, however, Kole felt no fear towards Nettle or for the stranger's place in her world. "Where did you come from?"

Nettle said, "I am from the lands of Sceanth. It is a place of rivers and of woodland creatures who ease our minds of troubles. Nymphs and imps and satyrs."

"Nymphs?" Kole scrunched her brow. "And how did you find yourself here?"

With one hand, Nettle anchored herself to the mantle; she felt the roughness of the wood, and then once again tapped on the pointy shrine upon its cup-shaped base with a single fingertip. "I dreamed in my life vein cocoon. I dreamed as I always do."

Stepping with discretion around the faerie in her home, Kole readjusted the shrine back into place with care. "And what is it you seek, Nettle? What brings you to the dismal shores of Erw?"

"I am drawn to your ocean. I've followed its crashing waves through the obscuring fog, and they have brought me to your home. Is it close? The ocean…am I close?"

With a near-silent snicker, Kole pointed a finger to the window. "Right out there. You'll never see it though, not with that damnable sea smoke."

"Sea smoke?"

"It looks like fog, but it spews forth from the ocean itself. It infects us all. Gets in our heads. Drives us to madness."

"And what of everyone else in this village? Where are they?"

"Again, the sea smoke."

"You blame the ocean for that, also? For the absence of people? Are you the only soul to be found here?"

Kole picked up the muddy boot and placed it along the base of a wall, reuniting it with its match. "The ocean takes what it wants from us and hides what we wish to see. The last of my village disappeared mere days ago. Most have been missing for weeks. Months. But they'll be back soon. My parents. They will return."

There was a sense of lies in the air. No matter what assurances were tossed her way, Nettle intuited that Kole did not really believe in her own words. And when it came to truths, Nettle was not one to allow falsity to persist. Certainly, Brawn could attest to that. "Will they?" she questioned.

Kole sneered impudently. "Best to be on your way, stranger from another land. Your precious ocean will never be found if you keep up the chatter."

Hmph, thought Nettle. Surely the ocean would not stray. "Then exit I shall," she said. She wanted to say something more to Kole, something about impetuous actions and choosing life veins, but it was best to leave on moderately amicable terms, rather than find herself at the wrong end of another boot, she thought.

Kole's stony face betrayed her feelings, though; a certain sadness and a grim portentousness were bubbling behind her gray eyes. Nettle motioned toward the still-open door, thinking of Brawn once more, and realizing it was the second exit she was making in two days, in two different worlds, and from two separate beings who appeared to be left with nothing but poisonous feelings toward her.

CHAPTER
4

IN NETTLE'S WORLD, IN THE GREEN LANDS OF SCEANTH, there are no surface oceans. At an unknowable distance below the crust, however, lies one that is buried. One only ever described in whispers and folk tales. Many of the creatures inhabiting Sceanth were afraid of it. Some yearned for it. Most were simply ambivalent toward it. A few knew nothing about it at all. The satyr Brawn once promised Nettle the ocean, and that he would take her to it at some point in their future. He built up the possibilities of this ocean in Nettle's mind, dizzying her senses with tales of its vastness, descriptions of its exotic, never-before-seen marine life, and reciting passages that paid homage to it, claiming to have once read from the sacred tomes of Ferron the Tallwood himself. The truth was, Brawn had never read a word in his life. And he didn't particularly believe in the underground ocean himself.

Lies aside, Brawn did have his moments of being good for Nettle. He did love her, in his own way.

He grew and cultivated the strangest yet most wonderfully

unique orchids in hidden spots behind his home and would always surprise Nettle with one when the memory of the previous flower had just expired. He once wrote a song for Nettle and fearlessly performed it before an unsuspecting crowd of imps and nature spirits in a forest clearing. He even painted her portrait on the side of an old oak tree on blistering afternoons when there was nothing else Nettle wished to do but return to the faerie enchantment field and avoid the heat.

But Brawn also promised her the ocean, even if they both knew he could never give it. And yet, Nettle wished for nothing more than to believe the satyr's words. She carried her wishes along with her inside her life vein cocoon and dreamed she might one day wake to discover the ocean, convinced it was the one thing that held the promises of a truer love.

Nettle wound her way between the dark spaces of more homes in the fishing village, coming ever-nearer to the one thing she could not have in the lands of Sceanth. There was a handmade wooden pathway that led to a rocky shore. Nettle reached for a slippery stone at her feet and licked it carefully with her tongue. It tasted like nothing she'd ever known; a flavor her tongue wanted to place. She inspected the curious, molar-like barnacles before replacing the stone precisely where she'd found it.

Unfolding her wings again, she fluttered above the beach toward the melodic lapping of waves. The rocks gave way to glassy sand and its heavenly collection of shells, crab carcasses, and kelp. But she ignored the urge to inspect them all individually; her goal was near.

Nettle landed softly, and her toes quickly melted into the fine, wet sand. A wonderful feeling of being tethered to this new world overcame her. It was not completely unlike the silt in the rivers of Sceanth. Much, much colder though. The waves rolled in, and the frothy, foamy, viciously freezing saltwater gathered around her shins. The cold water had an unpleasantness about it.

As the waves rolled back out again, she dipped a hand into the ocean and tasted the water from her fingertips, closing her eyes for a moment to take in the beguiling flavor; it had an unsettling saltiness and a wonderful pungency that lingered beneath her tongue.

But, most surprisingly to Nettle, it did not taste at all of love.

If anything, it was the exact opposite.

When she opened her eyes, Nettle was bewildered by the form the sea smoke had taken around her. It was difficult to distinguish, but there was a definite malevolence to it, like some trickery was at play.

Nettle fluttered above the water and followed the shoreline for a few minutes. A half hour. Longer, maybe. Time was holding less and less meaning in Erw. Eventually, she came to a burial ground of ancient fishing vessels; they were rotting, peeling, cracked, tipped on their sides, and even broken into pieces. A colossal collection of great skeletal beasts, too broken to carry on, too heavy to be moved elsewhere. Here, the shoreline was rimmed with a half-dozen of them. Anchor chains stirred the ocean water like a faerie's dipped finger might circle lazily in the river, lost in daydreams. The rusted metal created a fearsome, haunting sound. She wondered if this graveyard was where the missing villagers might have disappeared to.

Just as Nettle settled her feet again into the cold, wet sand, the wind picked up. Bells and chimes clanged in the distance. The spaces between the tide's rhythmic lapping upon the shore grew shorter and the ocean crept past Nettle, reaching ever farther inland. There was an intense power in this water that was stymieing her senses, sapping her strength, and making her feel far more powerless and insignificant than she was comfortable with.

From somewhere through the wind or within the waves, Nettle heard a deep breathing.

Then, much like the one that woke her from her earlier nightmares, a woman began screaming. Wailing. Tearing the sky in two. But this time, there was nothing to wake from. Nettle's teeth clattered from the assault. She could do nothing more than press her palms to her ears and clench her eyes tight.

When she opened them again, the sea smoke had dissipated some. The din had quieted, also: waves tempered, winds quelled, and bell chimes dwindled to nothing. Amidst the ocean's silence, Nettle spotted a dark figure in the water. Someone in a small boat, rowing slowly and methodically with a pair of oars. A pale blue glow surrounded them, barely flickering, as though the boat held a candle made of some wind-resisting magicks. The shadowy outline was becoming lighter, more ethereal, as it pushed its way out farther.

"Hello!" Nettle called, to no avail. She tried another glittery flare from her fingers in the hopes of garnering attention, but this proved to be fruitless, also. The lone figure in the boat disappeared into the distance without an answer. Nettle considered the otherworldly forces at work and what exactly was attempting to lure her beyond the shoreline.

Her feet left the beach and the faerie fluttered out over the water.

Time crawled slower. Her senses felt dulled. Only her own heavy breathing and the sloshing of oars in the water from somewhere not far up ahead reached her ears. Nettle almost stopped. A certain solicitude surrounded her, one that cautioned her to turn around, to return to the ghostly fishing village with the angry girl, rather than continue farther into the impending abyss. Nettle would have called out to the unseen figure again, but she knew for certain it would be futile. If mysterious figures wished to be unfound, they would remain so. On the other hand, if Nettle was meant to spot and accompany this soul into the ocean's misty nothingness, then there could only be the inevitable discovery. Her wings told her she had to keep pushing.

Another shape began to take hold. It was a small island, not far out. From its jagged, fang-like silhouette, Nettle could tell it was a wooded island; the distant scent of cedar and other deciduous trees helped establish its landscape also. Something else was there, too—somewhere under the brush, within the trees themselves, beneath rotting bark.

As she drew nearer still, the tallest point on the island began to reveal itself. Upon a plateau-like tower of rock, Nettle made out the shape of a woman, her arms stretched upwards; but she was only visible for an instant before the sea smoke obscured her again.

Still with no sign of the mysterious figure in the boat, Nettle approached the shore—a shore that was lacking the delicate sand of the fishing village, being nothing more than sharp rocks and shattered driftwood. The splashing tide grasped upwards through the cracks between rocks. She settled the pads of her bare feet onto some mossy stones. Twisted roots wound themselves amongst the land, which stank of rot and mold.

Nettle felt a tension in the air, simmering, as if any number of bad things were possible here.

And yet, even through the persistent sense of dread, there was a reassuring calm: a single stem of bright violet bluebells grew from the immediate outskirts of the thick, creeping brush. The bulbs hung showily, defiant towards the darkness lying just ahead. Nettle took a couple of the tepals into her gentle hand and thought immediately of the never-ending fields of Sceanth bluebells she had breathed in every morning. This bluebell was no different, sharing the same redolence; it was perhaps a bit brighter hue, though this could have been due to the contrast of its murky, joyless surroundings.

She almost plucked the bluebell from the ground, maybe in an attempt to rescue its beauty, but chose to leave it instead. This frightening shore on this terrible island might just need the flower more than she.

The thin wings of bluebell faeries were not strong enough to flutter above treelines for long, but Nettle's intuition suggested she might do well to avoid the darkness of the wooded island. Aided by the glow from her wings, she found her way to the highest point, where she'd previously spotted the woman with arms raised to the sky, as if summoning the night's incoming storm. Upon getting closer and seeing it from the proper vantage point, however, Nettle realized it was only a tree.

But a tree unlike any she'd ever seen before.

It was massive and black as space, as though it might create its own shadow even with an absence of light. Nettle could see her reflection in its sheer surface. Not quite bark; but something similar. Its exposed roots appeared to be melting over the landscape. What Nettle had originally perceived as arms raised upwards, were the tree's thick branches, oddly straighter than star beams. It grew no foliage whatsoever.

Aggressive waves continued to crash below her, with a growing intensity that made Nettle brace herself on the tree. She'd never known nature to feel this way. Something about the tree scratched at her insides. She peered closer into her reflection and noticed it was not her own. Familiar, but unrecognizable. Whatever it was, she looked away, not wishing to see herself from the strange tree's distorted perspective.

Within the darkness of the tree's skin, there was the shadow of an opening. A hole. Keeping her arm from being too far inside the hole, she felt the space with her hand, waving it around some in an attempt to gauge the size of the fissure. It was large; large enough for the slight body of a young faerie to slip through. Not so unlike the cavity she left open in her life vein cocoon.

Without much thought at all, Nettle squeezed herself inside the monstrous tree.

Nettle shook her head, freeing her mind from the thoughts of any safe havens back home. They would do her no good here in this world. The pitch-blackness within the tree seemed to absorb everything at once; no outside light—though nebulous as it was—seeped inside, and even the jittery sound of Nettle's trembled breathing was dulled to nearly nothing. A low moaning could be heard, but Nettle convinced herself it was merely the waves crashing around her; choking the island, like two sinister hands might crumple a piece of paper into a ball.

Her wings' glow illuminated the space only a little, enough to notice a tunnel that led downwards, seemingly beyond the monstrous roots, deep into the island itself.

Planting her feet upon the edge of the tunnel, Nettle felt a deep, subterranean hum. Something was alive down there. Nettle took one uneasy step, then another. She must have only crept a dozen more steps before realizing her innate glow had disappeared altogether. Worse, her acute senses were no more, and she could no longer sense dangers in the darkness. The humming though, whatever its origins, had only intensified.

But still she continued on, deep into the oppressive tunnel. There was a wind now, too: a slight, freezing gust from somewhere remote. Though it scared her, Nettle wanted to know where it led.

All the while, something else elected for her to tread no farther.

It was sudden, swift, and resolute. Something clobbered Nettle in the black space of wherever it was she'd found herself, stopping her breath mid-gasp and knocking her unconscious.

CHAPTER

5

First, she woke in the shadows beneath a bed. In a bedroom, in an old wooden house. Like the one she woke in when she first woke on Erw. It did not appear to be the same house as before, however, as the smell and the taste of the room's staleness were much different. Faded. Absent. The house creaked with its age and weather-worn condition. Nettle pushed a palm to the floor, partly to make sure her presence was real, but also to feel the life of the wood groan and strain within her. Once she was satisfied, she squirmed out from under the bed, opened her wings and flew to the window; outside was nothing but a black void. Not sea smoke or the night's darkness, but simply black. Black as the tree she'd crept inside. It was as though the tree was lurking just behind the glass, watching her, but this time there was no reflection of herself within it. In fact, everything was absent: the patter of rain; the distant static of the ocean's waves. The house had the same design as the one she'd woken in before—the place she was born into Erw—and Nettle floated along the same path, downstairs to the foyer.

Here, the state of the house was more decrepit, with frayed curtains, splintered holes in the floorboards, spider webs and scuttling bugs in every corner. The rusted scent of old nails sticking out of the wood, bent at every angle. A crooked bookshelf held books of mostly forest green and brown, bruise-colored spines. There were broken, empty picture frames piled on the floor and some nautical maps on the walls. A familiar detail called out to her: a single picture hung on one wall, and Nettle was drawn towards it. It was a charcoal drawing, and its subject matter was a small, wooded island. Choppy ocean waves were rendered mid-splash upon the steep, rocky sides. At the island's peak was a large black tree, stretching up into an ominous sky.

Nettle recalled seeing the same picture in the first house. And though she was certain there had been a second drawing hung next to it before, she could not recall what it was.

She hesitated for a moment before reaching for the picture. Carefully, Nettle lifted it from the wall. It was heavy—heavier than it had any right to be—and it was simultaneously freezing cold and hot to touch. There was a sudden pain, and Nettle wished to smash it onto the floor, but she could not find the will to let go.

The tree screamed in her mind. Nettle screamed back at it. She wanted to scream so hard she might light the awful tree on fire.

And then the picture did just that. It burst into flames, taking Nettle and the entire house with it. Leaving nothing but echoing terror behind in the marshy woods, and a horrible cackle that reverberated through the heavy sea smoke and back out into the ocean's depths.

Now she woke again. Still not within the blackness of the tree, and not beneath a bed in the house in the woods either. It was a cave. Nettle had woken in dark caves before, but there was something quite different about this one.

She was underwater.

And there was something very different about *her* now, too.

The murky, near-nothingness of the undersea cave barely gave way for the faerie's amber-pink glow, as Nettle tried using her ambience as a lantern to find a way out. Her faculties acted oddly: noises were warbled, her breathing felt abnormal, and her sense of smell did not work as it once had. Yet, Nettle knew intuitively she was in the ocean. It was alive in her mind and speaking words she could not comprehend.

Her body moved differently in this place, and when she finally pulled her senses together enough to question why, the ocean told her everything she needed to know: Nettle was no longer a faerie from the bluebell fields of Sceanth, but she was now, somehow, a mermaid from the ocean depths of Erw.

Mermaids did not exist in Sceanth, though there had been plenty of creatures who lived their lives in the sparkling rivers which divided the lands and flowed between them, creatures like the undines, the water nymphs, and the river hounds. There were also the dark creatures Nettle had never encountered— perhaps just stories forebears scared their little ones with—such as the turtle-shelled klinnim, who would rend limbs from un- wary passersby and wash the severed appendages in their rivers before consuming them, arm by arm and leg by leg.

She opened her hands and looked inside them. Nettle's eye- sight remained heightened, and even in the underwater cave she could see a slight, thin webbing between her fingers, and the lines on her palms had smoothed to an uncomfortable but slightly wonderful nothingness. From her fingertips, she tried to generate her defensive, pulsating light, but nothing happened aside from her own glow dimming a little from exhaustion.

With some hesitation, she reached under her thin dress and felt the tail with her hands. There was a thickness to it, but also an exquisiteness. She tickled herself a little upon its scales and the whiskery fibers that grew sporadically along its length. Swirling the water around, this new part of her was frightening. She could feel powerful muscles that had not been in her body before.

Whatever magick this was, it was either the work of another dream, or the result of entering the black tree.

Behind her, there was a murky glow seeping into the cave, the light like blood from a fresh cut immersed in water: a crack of an opening into the ocean's depths. With her tail, Nettle pushed herself towards it, but she stopped at the sight of the tree once more: it was growing downwards from the ceiling of the cavern. Black as a nightmare, its branches appeared to be reaching out for her. Grasping. Clawing.

But the lure of the ocean's unknown oblivion had greater power than even that of the tree's, and Nettle observed its call. She swam quickly, away from the suspended tree and out through the slight mouth of the cave.

There was much less sea life on the ocean floor than she would have suspected; some stringy, ethereal organisms floated past, while grayish weeds languished lazily in the seabed. Death found its way down here, too: bits of bones and rusted leftovers from long-ago shipwrecks. Nettle swam away from it all, her tail propelling her upwards toward the surface. Nettle's dress was starting to become a water-logged hindrance, so she pulled it off. The dress floated off for only a moment, before an angry current snatched it away somewhere unseen. Far above her there was light, and a strange pattern was cut into that light. She could not yet make it out, as the ocean continued to play with her senses; from a shimmering crosshatch glare to a puzzling veil of shadowy shapes—skulls, wings, and swirling vortexes. The torrent became choppier, alerting Nettle that she must be far away from the shore.

Still, Nettle swam closer to the surface. Closer until there was a black rectangular shape above her: the bottom of a boat. She paused beneath the vessel for a moment, considering its place in these waters and if it held a crew of any sort. The fisher girl's missing family, perhaps? What was the girl's name again? Nettle could no longer recall it.

Touching the wood of the hull, Nettle sensed its age and its substantiality. It smelled as wonderful as the ocean itself. Algae, mussels, undaria, and tunicates littered the bottom, like a colorful collection of ocean oddities. With her tongue, Nettle touched a frill of seaweed, but it tasted of nothing but slime and saltwater. Her senses could not detect the seaweed's place in the world nor in the expanse of Erw's ocean, not its distinct language nor its thoughts or desires. It was merely seaweed growing from the bottom of a fishing boat, and it shared no special connection at all with Nettle.

She did not like the feeling of isolation.

It was just as she was lost in thoughts of solitude and detachment from nature that the trawling net came down from above, bursting through the water's surface and ensnaring her instantly. Nettle screamed, though nothing came from her. She clawed at the netting, but her smooth hands were not capable of freeing her. Her tail's threshing only served to tangle her further. The ocean did nothing to save her. In fact, the tide's fury seemed to cease, and it was not long before the trawl began rising back to the water's surface. Voices above shouted victory in colorful tongues.

Nettle tried to wake herself, but there was no waking from this. She wanted to go back and listen again to her mother's omens about carefully choosing life veins. She wanted to *really* listen this time. She had to know what madness this was, and how to retrieve herself from it. "Your dreams will only worsen," her mother warned. "You must dissolve your cocoon—*destroy* it—before the threats it poses destroy *you*." She wanted to take back the times she dreamed in order to escape. She wished to discern the patterns of the growing bluebells. She reconsidered her feelings for Brawn. Her incomplete love for dear, sweet Piper. Nettle hoped she might see Piper again.

She hoped for many things.

And as she hoped, a massive shadow approached from below. The ocean screamed a dissonant roar in Nettle's mind. Before she could piece together what was occurring, the trawling net was torn from its chains and was once again fully submerged in the water. The boat rocked violently above. Some barrels and harpoons and brown glass bottles dropped into the torrent.

Nettle should have been hysterical, fearful, but she could only stare in awe at the murky form before her as the once-threatening fishing net billowed delicately around her like an aura: it was an ocean serpent of some sort. And although it was webbed in shadow, its sheer size had a gentle quality to it. The serpent was not here to destroy her, but to save her instead.

Nettle motioned towards the great beast, but it slithered beyond her reach. She could sense its *own* fear. Closing her eyes and opening her palms, Nettle focused her energy. Her glow intensified; her hands became soothing beacons for the creature, and it came closer, out from the darkness of the ocean's shadow.

Its fangs were many, with large teeth layered before larger ones, before even larger. It hungered for something, though just what it might feast upon could only be imagined. A black tongue hovered forgivingly within its open jaws. Nettle could not make out whether its scales were green, blue, or a shade of gray—not because of the ocean's darkness but more because the colors seemed to change endlessly. It was gargantuan, likely triple the size of the fishing vessel still rocking madly above. Its body was that of a snake; its two sinewy arms and magnificently taloned hands were more like those of the worst of demons and certain creatures lying in wait on the edges of terrible nightmares. But the serpent's red eyes had a chatoyant luster to them, enough for Nettle to know their flickering meant she was safe in its presence.

Nettle's glowing hands drew nearer, until she placed her palms upon its muzzle. They remained motionless for a long moment, each trying to sense the other's altruism and true intentions.

But again, it was merely a brief respite. From out of the serpent's massive maw, something came. It was a hand, then two—grayed and craggy, tipped with wretched nails—and they reached for Nettle's unsuspecting throat. So fast, Nettle did not notice until the hands of evil were already choking the very life from her, tearing her from her spot in the sea, and reeling her into the serpent's jaws. Screaming all the way, until she was devoured and forgotten.

Only some bubbles remained, floating up to the surface before softly popping from existence.

Finally, Nettle woke on a rocky outcropping at the water's edge. The briny saltwater scratched her lungs and throat, a stinging realization her body was no longer that of a mermaid's, if ever it had been. The cold, wet dress clung to her, obviously having never been lost at sea.

She had sudden doubts now, whether the ocean was really the one thing she'd always sought. Stories her father told—of the ocean's immeasurable beauty—rattled through her mind. She recalled that sparkle in his eye as he told tales of this thing he'd never once acknowledged, before gifting a human and returning home only sporadically. What had her father seen that changed him so?

The ocean scared her now. Surely Brawn would be pleased to know that much. She only wanted to find a way out, away from its pull. Not once had Nettle experienced the cold, creeping feelings like what she'd been feeling here. Erw's smudge of sea smoke blackened and stained her soul; it unsettled her thoughts, and it was beginning to unravel her mind.

Nettle found herself wanting to smash a jar of juni water upon her own life vein cocoon at the next chance she got, in order to dissolve it. She thirsted for the destruction of the one thing that ever brought her the joy of escaping to somewhere else. Still coming to her senses, Nettle asked herself: "Have I chosen my life vein poorly?"

The stink of caught fish was strong enough to indicate she was likely back near the fishing village. A seabird was pecking at some half-dead crustacean beside her. The light, even as murky gray as it was, hurt her eyes. She strained to see the figure standing over her.

It was the girl from the village, Kole, watching the life return to the faerie's strength-sapped body, and holding a hand out for her to take.

CHAPTER

6

As the door pushed open, the entirety of the dark, vacuous hall seemed to breathe in; the room held its breath, waiting to see what sort of danger the girls might bring with them. Nettle felt the opposite however, like any danger to be had would be lying in wait somewhere within the moldy, creaking walls. Thankfully, Kole's presence was now more comforting than hostile.

"Go on," Kole said. "Have a seat here." The hall appeared to have been used for town meetings, feasts, and other such village gatherings. Four long tables with equally long benches of heavily varnished driftwood filled the space. Lanterns that looked like they hadn't been lit for years hung above each table, swinging like some ghostly presence was floating around the room. As Nettle sat, Kole lit one of the lanterns with an unseen flame. The lantern swayed above them, its light casting a queasy, back-and-forth glow throughout the room.

Neither wished to speak first, but Nettle finally gave in. "Thank you again for bringing me here."

Kole still eyed the stranger curiously, but no longer found reason for a raised weapon to defend herself. "Earlier this evening, you left here in a hustle, anxious to find your precious ocean." She reached up, and touched the lantern softly with a hand, putting a stop to the swinging. "I'm guessing you found *something* before I found you on the beach. But my own experiences tell me that *something* could have been nearly *anything* at all."

"I don't know what it was. I remember seeing a boat. Following it. I went…I went inside a cave. And then—"

Kole paused, not fully understanding—maybe not quite believing—and hoping for more information. "And then—?"

Nettle rubbed the back of her head, still throbbing from whatever it was that struck her in the cave, deep beneath the black tree. She looked back to Kole with her big, wet, iridescent eyes. "I had visions…dreams. At least, I *think* they were dreams. Terrible, whatever they were. Then I woke up on the beach. I saw you there, and thought—"

"You think it was *me* who attacked you, don't you?"

"It would not have been the first time tonight you'd done so."

The girl shook her head a little, perhaps denying the accusation, but possibly also frustrated with the situation they'd both found themselves in, having crossed paths twice now. "Let me fix you a drink," Kole said with a certain amount of compassion, a definite switch from her earlier attitude of sheer indifference, with a little bit of bubbling trepidation.

"Just water, please." Nettle said. "Nothing stronger."

"Water? Is this what you find comfort in on your world, Nettle?"

"For me, yes. Well, dew water, if you wish to know."

"Right. I'll just fetch you some water then." She rose from the table, but stopped before entering the adjacent room, likely a pantry, and turned back to Nettle. "But try not to think about the ocean until I return, okay? I've found it can sometimes be bad to think about it too much."

It was an odd request, but Nettle gave her a nod in return,

nonetheless. With that, Kole exited the room, leaving Nettle alone once more. She heard the not-too-distant waves outside—mocking her, perhaps? chiding her?—and could not help herself from thinking about it further. Shadows appeared to move independently. She looked at her hands, to the palms and backs and palms again, and willed herself to create her familiar glimmer. The flare was much more dull and faded than it should have been, but her power *was* returning. After being unable to light her path inside the sinister island's shadowy tree, it was a relief.

Nettle did not hear Kole's return to the room but sensed her at the open door. The faerie hid her hands instinctively, but Kole either didn't see the dim light, or she was not shaken by the presence of such magicks. She reached over and placed two glasses in front of Nettle: a large one filled to the top with water, and a smaller glass, which smelled of something far stronger. Each glass was cracked and chipped, worn heavily from years of use; they looked like they might shatter if grasped too strongly.

"It's no dew water," Kole said, motioning toward the taller glass. "But it should do the trick." With both hands, Nettle lifted the glass and gulped down nearly all of its contents. Kole's eyes widened. "Looks to me like you *should* try something stronger." She splayed shaky fingers, and with a palm on the table, inched the smaller glass a little closer to her thirsty visitor. "There are towns around here that make much better—and so much more potent—drinks than this. But this will still do the trick."

"Thank you, but no. The water will suffice."

Kole tilted her head inquisitively. "You are…an unusual creature."

Nettle wondered just how much Kole might've known about creatures such as her. She kept her wings retracted, trying her best to conceal what otherworldliness she could. Whatever the girl knew, Nettle wished to change the subject immediately. "Can you tell me more about your family? And what was it that happened to them?"

Kole was quick to snatch the smaller glass, and she drank it down nearly as fast as Nettle did the water. "It was the sea smoke."

The almost empty glass returned to the table with a heavy clunk.

"You told me before it was the ocean. You said the ocean takes what it wants."

"The smoke. The water. It's all the same to those of us who are helpless to it. But my family will return."

"You told me that, too."

"Do you not believe me, Nettle?"

"I've not yet begun deciding what it is I should be believing, and what I should not."

Kole inhaled deeply, taking a moment to appreciate Nettle's response. "That's smart. But I didn't attack you, if that's what you suspect. I merely found you out there on the shore. Gods know, I've not ventured out into that hellish water at all."

"How did you find me then? One moment I was inside a cave, and the next I'm back here on the beach."

"It was a…glow? Or something. I glimpsed a light near the shore, and there you were. Like the ocean spat you out. But there was definitely a faint glow around you." Kole swallowed hard. Nettle remained unmoved. "There's more. When you left here earlier, I followed you. Not for long. You ventured over to the boat graveyard. But then you flew. And I saw the wings." She gestured with a single finger in the general direction of Nettle's back. "And then you flew out over the ocean."

Nettle shifted a little in her seat. Maybe thinking another attack with another muddy boot was not outside the realm of possibility.

Kole's entire body softened. "They were *beautiful*," she added.

Beautiful? Brawn had called Nettle beautiful before, but he'd never uttered such flattery toward her wings. Initially, she presumed the satyr was merely jealous of her gift of flight, as Brawn would forever remain as grounded as his own heavy wooden throne. In fact, the truth was he hated her wings. Their vivid color patterns made him queasy. They hid her face when he wished to speak to her. They got in the way during coupling, and on more than one occasion he demanded she retract them from sight. Though he also disliked the feeling of the folded wings beneath her skin. They felt unnatural, he said.

Dismissing the idea with a wave of her hand, Nettle said, "It is only my *glamour* that makes you sense any such beauty."

Kole looked at Nettle differently than Brawn ever had. "Can I see them again?" she asked.

Nettle blinked slowly. Then she stepped away from the table, and under the lantern's gentle, flickering yellow light, she unfolded her thin, glimmering wings. And she stretched them a little, creating a flapping sound so faint Kole wasn't sure if she'd heard anything at all. Nettle's amber-pink glow illuminated her spot in the room, a wonderful bit of life in the cold, dusty hall. Kole had no words but smiled as she watched the wondrous light dance and sparkle along the chipped rims of the drinking glasses between them.

Nettle asked, "You don't have faeries in your land, do you?"

"Is that what you are? A faerie? No, there's no such thing here in Erw. At least, I haven't known of any." For a moment, they searched the space around one another with skittish eyes, unsure of what to say next.

"May I sit back down now?"

"Yes. Of course. I'm sorry." Nettle returned to her seat but chose to keep her wings withdrawn. Kole still could not pull her eyes away from them. "What did you mean by your *glamour*? Is that a faerie thing, too?"

Though the creeping sea smoke was still a cold divide between them, Nettle felt it nice to talk this way with Kole. It reminded her of time spent with Piper. "All fae use glamour, though we each use it differently. Oftentimes on purpose, but also unintentionally. It can make a person see or not see what they want." She paused, wondering what it was Kole thought she may have seen. Or what she *wished* to see. "Basically, my looks can be deceiving."

Kole paused, as though trying *not* to say a word right then, but instead replied, "I like them."

A sliver of sharp teeth appeared as Nettle smiled cautiously in return.

"You said something about dreams you had—? Before waking up on the beach?"

"I remember…yes. There was a house on fire. And the ocean, too…" Nettle gulped. "The ocean. And a serpent."

Kole's gray eyes widened. "You dreamed of the serpent?"

"I *saw* it. It saved me." The girls remained in their seats; Nettle was unsure why exactly, but she was now more comfortable with the table between them. The distance was good. Safer. "What is it?"

"It's more of a legend than anything. You must have stories like it in your world, I'm sure. The serpent represents *hope* for us. Our legends—and most everything else around here—begin with the ocean. Here on Erw, the waters destroy what we build and take from us those we love. Even worse, when the tides recede out farther than our eyes can see, that is when it speaks to us."

Nettle leaned closer on the edge of the bench. She brought a hand to her mouth. "The ocean speaks—?"

"In our heads. When we sleep, but more often when we don't. It tells us the most horrible of things, our worst fears and nightmares. I've already lost my family to it, but I know my deepest fears are worse than simply being alone. There are more terrible things inside me I don't even know yet, and that cursed ocean would tell me all of it if it could. I don't think I'm ready to find out what it is."

There was a fear and a sadness emanating from Kole. Still, the faerie did not move to comfort her. Nettle dwelled instead on Erw's ocean. And of her ever longing to find such a thing for reasons no less than love but realizing it might only hold an uninviting malevolence instead. "But the serpent brings hope? Is it not meant to protect you?"

"It returns when all hope is lost, so they say. Some claim they've seen it; its shimmering scales cresting the waves. Some consider it no more than a fable, spitting in the faces of those of us who do believe. They think the ocean's fury is naturally abated, and the legends of the serpent are like making stories from constellations. My entire village believes in the great serpent. Our fortunes and feasts are tied to its strength. But now…something keeps it away."

Nettle sniffed at the air, sensing something was amiss. It felt as if some force were closing in around them.

Kole continued. "But there's something more to all of this. It's simply not natural. It's not right. Even for a place as cursed as Erw." If there were any creatures around them, there was no indication; no distant screeches or howling of dark songs. There was no breeze to blow the lanterns or rattle the thin windows. Sea smoke continued to lurk with grim solicitude. Kole paused with an intensified unease herself. "We all find ways to keep hope alive, though." She pulled at the high neck of her sweater, showing Nettle the green tattoo which had, until then, only been peeking out.

What the faerie had previously presumed to be a lightning bolt or a twisted vine, was now clearly a serpent. The same as she'd seen in the ocean. The body of a snake, with two arms ending in taloned hands. The same creature that had saved her. The beast's tail ran from just below an ear, down to its fanged mouth upon the girl's clavicle.

Kole said, "The great serpent is how I choose to keep hope. Though I'm beginning to think its return will never come."

"Hope is something we really have no control over, Kole. My own hope is kept through dreams. The dreams I live while in my life vein cocoon. I hoped for the ocean."

"For *this* ocean?"

"I am beginning to wonder about that."

It was the first time Nettle mentioned her cocoon, but it seemed as if Kole didn't hear her words. Perhaps too distracted by thoughts of her own. Kole checked the contents of her glass, maybe looking for an excuse for something. She tipped it on its edge and took note of its remaining few gray-brown drops. "You know, if my family *were* still around, they'd see the Gods strip me for drinking this swill. Are you old enough to drink in your world?"

"In the lands of Sceanth, upon emerging from our life vein cocoons, bluebell faeries can do as we please. There exists no *'old enough.'*"

Wiping her mouth with her sweater, Kole stared blankly at the faerie and her strange words. "Must be nice," she said, though it was obvious the girl did not fully understand all of the faerie's words. "You are a very different creature from what I know here. But they say Erw is a place where the opposites of everything exist, so I guess that makes sense."

"Opposites?"

"More like darker versions, I suppose."

"Who says this?"

"Travelers, mostly. Trespassers. Or just people passing through."

The faerie's iridescent eyes widened inquisitively. "Myself? Am I simply a traveler, or am I a trespasser?"

Kole pushed the glass and what liquid remained within it to the side. "I'm not so sure now. Do you wish to return, Nettle? To your world?"

Outside, the sea smoke had thinned enough that the closest dwelling could be seen from the window, though this clearing gave Nettle no helpful indication of what her answer might be. "That which I seek, I am unsure. Whether it is a way back to my home, or if I am meant to discover the reason this ocean scares me so. I first believed it was meant to fill me with wonder instead. With *love*, too."

"Love—? That is something I am…*unfamiliar* with."

"Bluebell faeries know much about love. Though many still do not know much at all. Perhaps I am here to help *you*? To return your family to you? I am not yet sure."

"My family's return will not be up to you. This much I know."

"How can you be so certain? Are you not curious as to what makes an entire village disappear? Does it not pain you to be the only one to remain?"

Kole shifted minutely to one side. "I'm not the only one the ocean chose to leave behind in this hole."

There was heavy suspicion in the air, and Nettle held her hands out in front of her, stretching them and splaying her fingers as wide as she could, as if taking up as much space as possible in front of her would limit the amount of uncertainty. "I've not sensed anyone else here."

"You wouldn't. Eamonn has ways of making himself go unnoticed."

"Eamonn?"

Kole's fingers fidgeted upon the table, picking at its splintered edge, circling knots in the wood, and making strokes through the dust and dirt. "Yes. He was a shipbuilder in our village, but he's scurried off for reasons of his own."

"But you know where he has scurried to?"

"I do. And I think we should pay him a visit. If you'll allow me to help you, that is."

Nettle considered the girl's suggestion, searching for hidden motives with a squint of her glossy eyes. She gave a tentative, but gracious nod.

"Let's be off, then. But one more drink, first." Kole rose from the table quickly, leaving an unseen thought behind: a space in the stale air that contained Nettle's lingering thoughts of *love*.

CHAPTER
7

IT WAS A TWISTED, OVERGROWN PATH KOLE LED THEM
through, as though she was purposefully attempting to confuse
Nettle, to muddle the faerie's senses, so she would not be able to
find her way back to this place again. Or perhaps unable to find
her way back *out*. But Nettle was surely only building up these
thoughts in her head, for the fisher girl had seemed to genuinely
want to help her.

With Nettle's glow lighting their way, they ventured from
the darkened fishing village, up the hill of tall, dead grass, and
back down again. Across a rotted bridge, through a bog, and
into marshy woods. Mangroves reached crookedly like the
roots of pesky weeds, or warlock's fingers casting spells and
curses on encroachers. Strangely, there remained no sign of
a sun in Erw. Fewer creatures seemed to inhabit these dark
corners; their calls and scents and movements—in fact, their
very existence—dwindled to an eerie nothingness. Rotted and
broken branches in the trees above could be heard, creaking
and cracking, some breaking off and falling down through

the wooden latticework, tap tap tapping upon the forest's wet floor.

Once across some mossy logs, through ferns as thick as curtains, and just as any sign of a trailway vanished altogether, Kole finally came to a stop in a grove. "He is here."

With some concern, Nettle gazed around, sensing. "There is nothing here."

"It's one of his weird tricks. Eamonn thinks keeping his presence hidden is enough to protect him from those who might wish to find him. Of course, *I* know where to find him. And I know for certain no one else is even looking for him."

"If you believe in the absolute certainty of things."

"I do."

Behind her, Nettle heard more falling tree branches as they pitter pattered into the dirt. Perhaps it was the persistent unease that made her turn to see, but when she did turn around, Nettle jumped back a little at the sight of the massive, gnarled tree. It was not as massive or as black as the tree she encountered on the island, but she still found it hard to believe it had gone unnoticed until now. There were objects hanging from it which resembled windchimes, though they made not the ringing melody of chimes, but more like an agitated tapping and scratching.

They were bones. Stick-like bones fastened with frayed rope and dangling from branches above her, but also scattered upon the ground. Small bones which could have been from rodents or maybe fingers, large bones resembling legs of ruminant forest creatures or possibly even people, and every size of bone in between.

Nettle should have been able to catch the sour scent of death around her, but it smelled of nothing instead. If indeed this was the façade of Eamonn's surreptitious hidey-hole, she did not enjoy the prospect of journeying further within.

Thoughts of Brawn's own forest hideout flashed through Nettle's mind. Not any of the few happy thoughts, just the broken, frightening, and oftentimes hurtful ones.

Kole brushed some dead leaves off a flat stone with her

boot. Upon intensifying her glow, Nettle could tell the stone was actually more like a tablet; there was an unusual language inscribed in the rock, almost like hieroglyphs. Kole began shifting the tablet with her hands, and it moved aside with much less effort than Nettle presumed it might. She said, "It's not really rock, but some driftwood painted to look that way." A stone staircase leading beneath the forest floor was revealed. Some spiders and beetles skittered for new hiding spots. "Like I said, Eamonn's got tricks, but they're nothing more than cheap illusions."

Still, Nettle knew there was something unnatural happening. Bones hanging from a monstrous tree were merely one indication. Her senses should not have been muted in such a way. "Then why are we here? For what purpose do we seek this man of simple trickery?"

"Eamonn used to live in the village with us. But he left when his wife—when she disappeared."

"Taken by the ocean, too?"

"Aye. She was the first. But Eamonn also knows more about the realm of Erw than anyone. If you have questions regarding where you've been, what you've seen, or how you might return home, then he will help. He may even have answers regarding your connection to our ocean." Kole placed a trusting hand on Nettle's arm. The physical contact tickled the faerie.

They descended the stairs, Kole's shadow cast by Nettle's glow, quivering along the uneven walls of a dirt tunnel. Kole brushed some expansive spider-webs out of their way, an indication the passageway had not been used for some time. Dried clumps of trapped and long-dead insects in the webs offered only mild resistance. They reached the bottom and their feet pressed into wet soil. A door awaited them. There was no handle on it, no adornment whatsoever. The door smelled of the sea, and algae clung to its edges, though the wood was dry and had not seen water for ages. The hull of a fishing vessel, perhaps? Nettle could hear the passive *buk-bawk-bukawking* of a clucking bird within.

Kole announced their presence with a kick upon the door. Grass, dirt, and dried mud flew from her boot like spores blown from a dandelion. "Eamonn! It's Kole. I bring company."

From the other side of the imposing door, Nettle could make out the sounds of a body scrambling, weighty items toppling, and miscellanea shuffling. Then, finally, a reply. "Company? Do you also bring danger?"

Perhaps out of sheer predisposition, Kole scanned Nettle once more from the corner of her eyes. She concluded decisively, "I do not."

There was the sound of a heavy slab of wood lifting before the door itself creaked outwards. A face poked through the opening, though his was partly obscured by a ratty cloth over his eyes. "It *is* you," the man said to Kole. It was obvious he had not been accustomed to having visitors.

"I told you it was, Eamonn." She gestured toward her faerie companion. "This is Nettle."

"She's glowing!" Even through the cloth covering, he could detect Nettle's power. "And wings? Is she a pixie?"

"A faerie."

"Is there a difference?"

Finally, Nettle spoke for herself, defending her proper place in the world. Her glow intensified. "Pixies live amongst the Snippets of Thistlemoor. I am a bluebell faerie from the lands of Sceanth."

Eamonn questioned the bit of nonsensical information for a moment before nudging a bit closer, sniffing at the air around Nettle. "But she does not bring danger?"

The faerie's amber-pink glow softened. "I do not," she said, just as Kole had moments before. And before Eamonn could make a decision on the matter of having company, Nettle pulled the door open and fluttered past him. Kole followed close behind.

Inside was a small room. In one corner was a single table crowded with dusty trinkets and peeling books; in another was a pile of old bones. There was a tiny, neatly made bed. Eight large stones sat at the foot of the bed, keeping the lengthy covers pinned to the floor. Tapestries hung on Eamonn's walls, like he was more of a king in a castle and less of a hermit in a hidden shack. A chicken scratched across the floor, its head down and out of view. Two ravens—one of black and one of pure white—were perched upon a high chair back. For someone trying to stay hidden, it seemed counterintuitive to keep noisy birds in their home. The animals were content to keep to themselves, though the ravens did eye Nettle closely.

The stranger stood silently as Nettle took in the details of his home, including those of the man himself. Eamonn was taller than the two girls—and much older—and he had a muscular build, presumably from years of ship building, as Kole had mentioned. He was dressed similarly to Kole, wearing a wool cap, a high-necked sweater, and pants grown heavy from years of exposure to the salt spray of the ocean. With dirty fingernails, he scratched deep into his thick, scraggly beard. His other hand pulled at the curious cloth wrapped around his eyes, tightening it from behind. On the back of one hand, peeking out from the cuff of his sleeve, was a green tattoo similar to the one on Kole's neck. Another hopeful believer in the great serpent of Erw.

Finally, Eamonn broke the silence. He turned back to Kole and asked, "What does the faerie want from us?"

With her back to him, Nettle answered, "You may speak *to* me, rather than around me." The man's disdain toward her reminded Nettle of one of the many ways she could be treated by Brawn. She pinched a thumb and finger together. "Show me *this* much respect, Eamonn, and I will show you the same."

Eamonn moved to the chair with the two perched ravens, and sat down. His movements were slow and calculated. "Though I mask my eyes, I am certainly not blind. My apologies if I've angered you."

Nettle raised a sharp finger between them. "Then might you remove the blindfold? I am not comfortable with the distance it places between us."

"I wear this blindfold to mask my presence. To obscure my place in this world."

"Mask your presence? From what?"

Eamonn paused. "Likely from the very things you've come to see me about?" He turned to Kole, looking for some sort of confirmation, but she only shrugged her shoulders a little.

The chicken pecked at the pile of bones in the corner while the ravens continued to watch Nettle curiously. "The ocean troubles me," she said. "It draws me into itself, though it seems to also reject my presence. I do not know if Erw wishes me here."

"And yet—?" Eamonn asked.

"And yet, at the same time, I do not know if I wish to return to Sceanth. What I seek—what I *thought* I sought—I have not yet found."

From the chair, Eamonn reached across the table and took an object in his hand. It appeared to be wrapped in the same cloth as the one that covered his eyes. Something shined through the fabric. "Is it *love* that you seek?"

"Do we not all want the same? In some form or another?"

"That is all too true, faerie. This land you came from? Sceanth? Does it hold dark memories? Great sadness?"

Nettle stopped. Though she appeared to be thinking over the hermit's question carefully, she was really pausing to find the strength to answer. It was thoughts of her father that were holding her back. Of Brawn. And Piper. She wished they'd have begun to fade, but her life on Sceanth—her waking life, if this were really still a dream—remained at the forefront of her memories. As did the dysphoria she found while not inside her life vein cocoon. "It does," Nettle said.

Unwrapping the cloth, Eamonn was quick to cover the object again with his palms, maybe in the hopes it remained concealed from whatever outside forces he feared. The light emanating from the trinket continued to seep through the cracks between his fingers. The white raven didn't appear to like it, however, and it hopped onto the top of the bed.

"May I ask," Nettle began. "How might you help me? What is it that I seek here?"

Eamonn replied bluntly. "The Revenant, of course."

Nettle looked over at Kole, hoping for some meaning behind Eamonn's answer.

Kole watched both the faerie and the old fisherman, studying the two of them, and perhaps deciding her own place in things. Which side she was best taking. "A Revenant is a tree," Kole said. "The Obsidian Revenant, we call it. Though some say you can't see it. You *feel* it. You *dream* of it."

Immediately, Nettle was reminded of her journey to the hidden island; the one that ended with her entering the pitch-black tree. She told Kole it was a cave. Nettle asked her, "Is that what *you* believe?"

With a meaningless shrug of her shoulders, Kole looked back over at Eamonn. "The tree is no myth," he said from behind a shaking hand, fingers brushing unsurely in and around his lips. "I've seen it *three times* now myself. Harker had seen it many more than that."

"Harker?"

"My wife. She was drawn to the Revenant. Had a knack for just…finding it."

"But now she is gone, too?"

"Harker came here from the city of Porteous. She wasn't used to the wilderness, or the darkness of this place. And yet, she loved nothing more than exploring the spaces that were not meant to be explored. Some of her recklessness was passed on to me when the ocean took her away. Which is why I chose to leave. The things I knew only served to put our village in danger."

"Little good it did. Everyone is *gone* now, Eamonn."

Even from beneath the blindfold, the man questioned Kole with his eyes. "Everyone but you?"

"I wasn't there. I was at the shrine."

His brow furrowed. "The shrine? Or were you off in Yarari drinking again? Girl, there is no liquid cure for any of this in those taverns. There never has been."

"I was praying for the return of our boats and the men we'd lost. When I came home, the last of them had vanished. The women and children. *Everyone.* At first, I thought I'd returned to find myself trapped in a dream. But we always wake from our dreams. It's the nightmares that find a way to last forever. The cursed ocean only knows pain and destruction."

"Exactly the reason I choose to stay hidden."

"All of our vessels have been destroyed. Smashed to pieces!" As Kole spoke, Eamonn only clutched the object tighter. "Alone, I began work on rebuilding a boat. I didn't get far before it was consumed, too. My hands, bloodied and calloused for nothing. I could have used *your* hands. I needed your help! But you were hiding down *here*."

Eamonn removed his wool cap and discerningly placed the glowing object within it. He pushed the cap along the tabletop, out of reach. The white raven returned to its original spot on the back of the chair, behind Eamonn's shoulder.

Nettle had nothing to contribute to discussions of missing villagers or building boats. It was the matter of mysterious trees that continued to trouble her. "These trees—these Obsidian Revenants—I would like to know more."

Eamonn stood up tall; his blindfold and raised arms made him appear more like a crazed soothsayer than a man of purported wisdom. "First off, there is only a *single* tree. It grows somewhere unknown, though it has a knack for appearing wherever it wishes. For *whomever* it chooses. The Obsidian Revenant does its best to hide itself from us. Its black skin absorbs all light. No common soul can see it. Not really."

Nettle asked, "Not really?"

Eamonn paused for a moment. "I've seen it. It was long ago, I was still living in the village. I'd gone for a walk, to a spot I'd go often, when I was uncertain of my place here. We all have such a spot of our own. But this time…I believe it was the darkness that drew me there." He shuffled a few steps to face one of the tapestries on the wall—a blue-toned work of many swirling circles; maybe waves, maybe planets, maybe eyes watching. "One moment it wasn't there, and the next? Well, there it was, looming in front of me like a mountainside, reflecting my own face back at me." Eamonn touched his face, his beard, with tired hands, recalling the experience. "But it wasn't really *my* face, was it?" He paused and scratched the backs of his weathered hands now, looking for the best words. The right memory. "I wished to turn away, but I couldn't. All it seemed to want was to pull me in. And just when I thought it was over, I was saved. A girl, I remember her so clearly—her hair in immaculate braids, and even muddied I could tell her gown was elegant—she pulled me away from the tree. It was the first time I'd met Harker. I found it hard to turn my eyes from her beauty. When we eventually looked back, the tree was gone, having left only some foul-smelling sea smoke behind.

"It happened again later, this time at the Black Cliffs. Harker found it. In a different place but playing the same games with our minds. There it was, and then, there it wasn't. Just like that.

"The third time it happened I had come prepared; I carried a fisher's edge with me. A shell-splitter. When I saw the tree this time, I took a piece of it. I dug that splitter into its skin and scratched a sliver right out of it." Eamonn sat back down, doubling over a little and clutching his head as if in terrible pain of a memory. "The wail I heard! It haunts me still." The white raven jumped directly onto Eamonn's shoulder.

"I have also heard it," Nettle spoke. "The wailing. A woman's piercing scream." Eamonn's brow raised from behind his blindfold. "It was the kind of ear-splitting scream one does not wish for another to experience."

Kole asked Eamonn, "Where is the Obsidian sliver now? Do you have it still?"

The man pressed his lips together, curled them inside his mouth; again, his nails scratched at the backs of his hands. "I have it." Eamonn reached over to the other end of the littered table, past some cutting tools and rope, and he took another wrapped artifact into his hand. "Here," he said, unfolding the cloth. There was a black shard within; sparkling and absorbing the light around it at the same time. He offered it to the girls.

Nettle extended a hand carefully but did not take it. "You've gone to great lengths to conceal yourself, wizard. And yet you've brought *this* into your secret home?" The very presence of the tree—even if merely a sliver—made her uneasy. "What makes you presume the sliver ripped from an Obsidian Revenant isn't giving you away?"

Eamonn's lips clenched once more. He laughed a perfunctory breath out his nostrils. "I am no wizard," he retorted. "But my presence is secure, I can assure you of that."

Kole interjected, taking the Obsidian shard for herself. "Perhaps you need to unwrap more than this artifact, Eamonn, in order to see just how blind you are." The girl looked at it, turning it over again and again in her hand. "I've no doubt dark forces are out there. But hiding from destruction is no way to avoid it." With that, Kole tossed the bit of black tree back onto the table like it was nothing more than a dried out, empty bottle. It spun a couple of full circles before coming to a dead stop.

"I am still unsure of the reason why we've come here," Nettle said. "Your knowledge of this Obsidian Revenant is confounding at best."

Eamonn brushed some bird seed off the surface of a journal atop the table. "I write," he said. "I write about things that will happen."

"Prophecies?" Nettle asked.

"Not prophecies, no. These are events that have already happened, and *will* happen again."

"That sounds just like prophecies."

"It's cyclical. Just like my encounters with the great tree. Not unlike the ocean's destructive ways or even the witch herself."

"The witch?"

Eamonn turned to Kole sharply. "Did you not tell this faerie *anything* before bringing her to me?"

Kole shrugged. "Honestly? You're better at all of this than I am."

Taking a deep breath, Eamonn gathered himself and crossed his arms in front of his chest. "Here's the short version. Erw's ocean is a hostile, sentient force. When it crashes our shores, it does so out of pure malice, and nothing else. But when the sea's dark power becomes too much for us to endure, the serpent returns. It *always* does so."

Nettle asked, "And this witch?"

Eamonn tightened the blindfold, tugging at a knot behind his head. "The Erw Witch harnesses the sea smoke. She uses it to drive the serpent back."

"For what reason?"

"Reason? Not everything needs reasons, faerie girl. Surely you must know that, having seen what you've seen." He sat motionless, perfectly still for a moment, like he was unsure of how to put his next thoughts together. "It is like you said yourself: we all want the same, in some form or another. Even in a dark place such as this, love is a powerful, guiding force."

Again, Nettle thought of Piper. She wondered—if only briefly—whether Piper was thinking of her, too.

Eamonn continued, "There may not be *reasons*, but there are *answers* in the tree. I *know* it."

Nettle continued to put the pieces together. "But you can't find it again without going back out there. And you're afraid of surfacing, aren't you?"

Eamonn pointed at the chicken in the corner now. Still clucking and poking around in the pile of bones. "This is why I send *him*. The chicken's mind cannot be read."

"Because it is a stupid animal?" Kole asked.

Eamonn laughed. "Much simpler than that. It's because he has *no head*, of course." He snapped a finger and the chicken stopped for a moment before raising its neck. Indeed, it was nothing more than a headless, feathery stub. Though the preposterous creature still managed to make its *buk-bawking* clamor. "This is Talem. Talem will find the Obsidian, and through it he will find my wife. It is his destiny."

Nettle did not require the use of her powers—to lay hands upon the bird—to know that was likely not the case. Destiny was not something meant for animals such as Talem. Still, there was some kind of magick at play, keeping the headless chicken alive. The ravens of black and white continued to watch the faerie closely, almost corroborating Nettle's suspicions.

"And you two girls"—Eamonn continued, with a hint of something darker in his voice—"You who have come into my home looking for answers, will find them if you follow him."

Kole was matter-of-fact. "So, in order for *you* to survive, you hide down here, but it's okay for *us* to be out there?"

"You have the faerie," he said, this time intentionally speaking around Nettle. "It's obvious she has been brought to Erw for a reason. Her presence will keep you safe."

The two of them—the faerie and the orphaned fisher-girl—looked over one another carefully. Kole responded to Eamonn while keeping her eyes locked upon Nettle. "What if her reasons for being here are *not* so obvious?"

"I've realized I can no longer do this alone. The Obsidian eludes me. My wife is out there somewhere; I *know* she is." Eamonn moved towards Nettle, and brought a hand close to her, maybe feeling for a warmth from her glow. "I am just one star in the night, but no night sky is complete with a single star, is it? Only a constellation will guide us past the darkness." The two ravens flew to Eamonn's shoulders—white on the left, black on the right—and he addressed Nettle, Kole, and Talem as a group. "Find the Obsidian Revenant. Do what I cannot. And bring hope back to the realm of Erw."

One of them clucked in acknowledgement of the undertaking, speaking for the other two.

Meanwhile above, the sea smoke continued to roll through the darkening lands.

CHAPTER
8

WHEN THE HONEY-COLORED MOON SITS PRECISELY IN the center of the sky, and the air is sticky like spider webs and tastes of cinnamon and frost, this is when the bluebell faeries of Sceanth enter their second phase. In this span of time, each is tasked with creating their own life vein cocoons. The cocoons are unlike the silky casings commonly spun by larvae, and more resembling a many-layered, wooden shell; a perfect sphere, like an avocado pit, clinging to the underside of giant killorn tree branches. These are integral to the faeries' development, preparing them for their anticipated, though often feared, third phases. But the cocoons also serve as tools to help the faeries develop independence, individualism, and to realize their potential within the colony.

On the first day a life vein cocoon shows signs of cracking, the air reeks of nectar from the nameless fruits of the killorn trees. Only a tiny tear appears at first, but it isn't long before the cocoon is pulled apart from the inside. Slowly, sharp, pointed fingers pierce through the pillowy, fibrous membrane and the woody outer layer, like creeping ivy through cracks in a wall. One by one, the bluebell faeries emerge from their wooden spheres. Eggshell-like pieces of life vein cocoon husks fall from branches, and thump softly upon the bare forest floor as dozens of faeries celebrate their new beginnings, buzzing gleefully around the giant killorns.

Most faeries will abandon their life vein cocoons upon waking into their third phase. As is tradition, they will quickly fly to the nearby sacred spring, where butter-yellow lilies float on the surface year-long, then proceed to collect reeking juni water in tribute jars to douse their life vein cocoons, dissolving them into nothing.

But Nettle did not emerge as the others did. Not a line or crack upon her cocoon's surface. Nettle remained in her life vein cocoon for nearly three half-moons before finally choosing to emerge. And when she did, there were no other faeries flying with her; they had all moved along. Nettle was not ready to fully part with the dreams of her cocoon. Even as the wind carried the fragrances of juniper and elderberry to Nettle, she resisted their pull, choosing instead to relocate her mostly-intact cocoon. She moved it surreptitiously, from one spot to another, hiding it from her colony—but also from huntsmen and hungry creatures searching for ever more sustenance—far away from the bluebell fields, and closer and closer to the woodland den of her erratic satyr boyfriend, Brawn.

Nettle kept her life vein cocoon for reasons she was perhaps not wholly certain of, concealing herself from her own world in order to dream of other worlds. To maybe find the ocean that eluded her.

From within, Nettle experienced everything that could not be experienced on Sceanth. She wandered through forests incredibly lush and muggy, the moon nearly impossible to sense beyond impenetrable vegetation and vine-covered canopies. She visited towns full of people; the smallest of hamlets littered with medicinal remedy and hat shops, while the largest seemed full of bustling, impatient folks, and buildings of many stories stretching out forever into the skies. Her favorite, but most elusive dreams, were of ever-reaching oceans and the babble of sea life deep beneath their surfaces; the most incredible seashells appeared with every footstep along rocky beaches.

For other fae, after dissolving their cocoons, there is nothing left for them to do but boldly enter their third phase. They paired off and flew to wherever the scents and lights of Sceanth would guide them. Maybe for a half-moon; maybe two. Until the magicks of the land would summon them back to the bluebell fields.

With her secret tucked away, Nettle eventually paired off with other fae, too. First with the jumpy Soren, but he proved to be much too excitable about nearly everything. Next it was with Clementine, but one morning Clem went to pick berries too far past the Forest of Redd—where fearsome glimmer giants roamed—and she never returned. Later, Nettle found Clementine's basket, spat out of the Forest of Redd and lined with dried, still-sparkling juices and faerie blood.

Finally, when Nettle was drawn to the toads' glade by the scent of dewdrops on mushrooms and the taste of sticky sweet honeysuckle in the air, she discovered Piper had been drawn there as well.

She vaguely remembered Piper from when they were much younger, though Piper's second phase had done wonders for her. Where once she was a gawky, gangly thing who had difficulty flying and seemed to only attract bad smells and mosquitoes, time spent in her life vein cocoon had transformed Piper into something unearthly. She had a resplendent lime green glow around her, a honeyed voice that quieted crowds, and collar bones with the most sumptuous of curves to them.

Piper had also been holding on to her own life vein cocoon but admitted to Nettle that she was ready to dissolve it, if it meant the two of them being together. Nettle did not intend to lie to Piper, but told her the same, nevertheless. Every few nights, however, she flew in secret with the five-winged voros moths to her hidden cocoon on the outskirts of the satyrs' woods, where she would covertly continue to dream her way out of Sceanth.

Piper had no idea. When they were together, nothing else seemed to matter. They spent hours lying in the bluebell fields, gazing at the stars. They counted each one of them, and kissed every time they spotted a shooting star or an unexplained flare in the night sky. They kissed madly. They held one another like there would never be anything, or anyone else, to hold on to ever again. They spent every night that way; every night Nettle wasn't elsewhere in her hidden cocoon, that is.

And on one of those very nights, as she woke from a terrible dream—a dream that had taken her to a burning forest, with pixies and fae alike screaming and melting from existence—Nettle squeezed out of her life vein cocoon to find a wandering satyr outside, leaning against a tree. He was drinking something from a golden goblet worn to a dull hazelnut color.

"What brings a faerie so deep into my woods?" asked the curious nature spirit. The creature had the ears and tail of a horse, the legs, hooves, and juvenile horns of a goat, but otherwise quite human. And he spoke very well for someone of his moderately grotesque appearance. Having the innate glamour of a faerie though, Nettle knew of deceiving appearances, and was not immediately repulsed by his peeling skin, bulbous nose, or scruffy mane.

"I come here to hide," Nettle answered.

"And you hide from what? Trolls? Glimmer giants?"

"From my own, actually."

Without fear, the satyr approached the cocoon and rapped some calloused knuckles upon its rough, wooden surface. He inspected its near-impeccable craftsmanship, and even stuck his thick fingers into its opening while taking a gulp of whatever stinking potable filled his goblet. "You are a bluebell, are you not?" he asked with reeking breath.

"I am." She looked around, sensing the woods to be slightly more terrifying than she'd originally considered.

"You are beautiful," he said, without much thought, really. "I don't often see much beauty on my walks."

"That is absurd. There is beauty all around," Nettle noted.

"The colorful blooms at the foot of trees, the moss upon the branches, and even the red-bellied pang grubs beneath the stones."

The creature only huffed in disagreement. "I've grown tired of such paltry things. It is *you* that has piqued my interest on this day." The satyr stood as straight as he might. "I am Brawn."

The faerie had no reaction, other than removing Brawn's hand from her cocoon, pushing it away with her own. She shrugged her shoulders indifferently.

"You have not heard of me? Son of Fodpot, King of the satyrs?"

Nettle almost raised her shoulders again, but instead asked, "So that would make you a prince?"

"Indeed it would."

"I've still not heard of you."

"Alas, that does not make you any less beautiful, bluebell faerie."

"My name is Nettle. You may call me Nettle."

"And so I will." Brawn lifted the goblet towards her, offering a taste, but she was quick to decline.

"And *this* is your first offering? A sip from your filthy goblet?"

"I can give you whatever you dream. Nothing is impossible for me."

Nettle considered the limits of impossibility. "What of the buried ocean? Can you promise me the ocean, son of Fodpot?"

Brawn smirked. Something in his eyes flared. "If the ocean is what you dream of, the ocean is what I shall give you." He held the goblet up to the faerie once more. Nettle took a tiny moment to look back in the direction of the bluebell fields— somewhere in the far-off distance, obscured by knobby trees, overgrown toadstools, and a mist that wasn't there a moment ago—before taking a sip of the satyr's pungent drink.

Piper was in the river when Nettle returned the next morning, dipping her hands into the languid current, pulling out stones.

She inspected the river's rocks often, fascinated by their unique colors and various degrees of erosion. Nettle carried a cobalt blue orchid in her own hands, a gift given to her by Brawn, plucked from somewhere behind the massive tree that housed his den. She approached Piper slowly, her mind preoccupied with thoughts of her night spent in Brawn's bed, rather than in her cocoon. Rather than with Piper. A lie within another lie.

When Piper saw her, she dropped the stone back into the river and flew over to Nettle, arms wide open. "Where did you find that?" she asked about the orchid.

"It was in the woods," Nettle said. "In a spot I'd not visited before." She loved the way its strangely-curved petals tickled her wrist as she held it.

Piper reached her hand out for a closer look, though Nettle did not let it go. "It's striking. And a bit strange." She smiled and giggled a bit. "But that's how I like the objects of my affection." She kissed Nettle tenderly on the forehead. Nettle smiled a smile that hurt a tiny bit, in the corners of her mouth and in the pit of her stomach. She kissed Piper quickly on the lips to make it hurt a little less.

"Should we plant it in our garden with the others?" Piper asked.

Nettle looked closely at the orchid between them, and she worried about whether the taste of the satyr prince might still remain on her lips. "No. I think I'll keep this one separate." But Piper seemed none the wiser.

That night, as the two faeries held one another beneath the stars, and as she combed Piper's hair with her long, needle-like fingers, Nettle thought of Brawn again. Her heart skipped a beat and her wings fluttered uncontrollably, even as she traced a finger along Piper's magnificently-curved collar bone. And even still as the exquisite Piper settled into a deep slumber, and as the voros moths beckoned, hoping to return to the woods that concealed the life vein cocoon, Nettle disregarded it all in favor of the memory of Brawn's promise: that he would one day give to her the great buried sea of Sceanth. That she would one day feel the ocean.

Another phase passed. The moon had been stuck at a quarter-size for longer than it had only a few phases before, as though time itself was slowing. For all their cognizance of nearly all entities within the lands of Sceanth, the bluebell faeries seemed to pay very little attention to the moon. Nettle felt a strong connection with the moon, however, but even she was preoccupied now, balancing her relationships with Piper and Brawn, and also with recurrent time spent dreaming within her life vein cocoon. She continued to dream, even though her dreams—and the darkness they fed her—seemed to only be worsening.

As she'd always done, Piper made dresses and accouterment for the bluebell faeries, sewn from the giant leaves of killorn trees; the pieces intended for Nettle were intricately laced with golden strands of rare alder wire, of which she also used to weave crowns to be placed atop Nettle's head. Brawn continued to hand out ever more orchids—each one a never-before-seen color and shape—all the while incessantly stressing how his stubby horns would grow longer when his time as king began to draw nearer. Nettle's dreams were of shadowy, many-armed creatures pounding upwards through the earth. They grabbed her, destroyed her alder crowns, and tore the wings from her body. The creatures took the wings to their mouths and fed, slurping the amber-pink glow from them, before folding up the discarded appendages and placing them between pages of a massive tome—the book's paper made from faerie flesh, and bound in dusty, gray bones of the dead.

Piper learned how to meld her lime green aura with Nettle's own, a sacred and intimate ritual of the bluebells. She would perform elaborate dances, for the delight of all creatures in the bluebell fields: ladybugs, voros moths, and the rainbow-crested flitters. Brawn and Nettle would lay upon nests of pine needles, finding shapes above them within the holes in the forest canopy where sky would poke through, like finding shapes in the clouds. Hers would be optimistic shapes, while his would inevitably be cruel and hostile thoughts. Nettle's dreams were of barefoot and bearded men, their hands covered in dried blood, cracking open her life vein cocoon, and pulling her out in her sleep. While she remained helpless, these interlopers buried her body in a hole so deep Nettle thought she could actually smell the underground ocean beneath her; though it smelled as putrid as the liquid consumed from Brawn's goblet.

And Nettle's dreams worsened. She dreamed of thorny vines growing from her mouth, tentacle-like creepers unrooted her teeth as they burst from her gums. In horror, she watched her reflection in the hallowed mirror pool—thick, glittery faerie blood dripped into the still water and formed a craggly version of her own face. Her reflection cackled back at Nettle with teeth of her own: fearsome, jagged, and sparse.

Winter came suddenly, with a piercing freeze in the air and ice on the river. The whitest of blue-white snow hardened upon the forest floor and on the bare branches of the killorns. And even though the bluebell fields remained warm due to faerie enchantment, winter was enough to make the songbirds of Sceanth unwelcome, and they returned to their seasonal homes far beyond the Forest of Redd and over the Tower Mountains. Nettle couldn't help it, but when the whistling farrows and the rainbow-crested flitters were absent, she always felt a bit more alone. The birds were her friends and their songs invigorated her.

"I've heard of rainbow-crested flitters who live year-round in the satyr woods," Piper said one particularly crisp morning, when Nettle made mention of how much she missed their singing. The two of them were outside the reach of the faerie enchantment, seated close together upon a giant frozen toadstool watching their colony flutter within the bluebell fields. "The satyrs—those creatures are horrible..." She looked to Nettle for a reaction. ". . . But the satyrs' music is enough to keep the flitters from migrating further north. At least, that is what I've heard."

"I've not heard that," Nettle responded. She'd not once seen a songbird during her time spent in Brawn's woods.

"It was Shae who told me as much."

"Shae has always been a terrible liar, Piper. And I don't believe any creature to be so unquestionably horrible. Not even the satyrs."

Their bodies were not bothered by the cold, but Piper still squeezed herself in closer to Nettle. "How about we see if we can't find one, then?" Her lime green glow flared upon the mere suggestion. She was being far more audacious than Nettle was used to.

"A flitter or a satyr?"

"Take your pick. We'll venture into the woods and see what we see, I suppose."

Nettle did not know what Piper's intention was; whether she was truly up for adventure or if the sweet faerie knew more than she let on, daring Nettle to lift the veil upon her secrets. Nettle did love her though—some called it a great flaw of the bluebell faeries: that they fell in love too easily. Nettle loved Piper more than she'd ever loved anything that wasn't an ocean dream, so she told her about her life vein cocoon hidden in the satyr woods. She didn't destroy it as Piper had destroyed her own; the worlds within the cocoon were much too intoxicating. And as horrible as they could sometimes be, her dreams were the only things she was ever sure of. With absolute certainty.

"More than you're sure of me?" Piper asked.

Nettle gulped a heavy gulp. "It's not just you and my dreams taking up the corners of my mind, sweet Piper. It's more than that." There was a creaking and cracking of the tall, snow-tipped ash trees towering above them. "There's more."

"It's the satyr prince, isn't it?"

"So, you know of Brawn?"

"Nettle, his father is the king of the satyrs! They are an irrational, deranged people. If he felt like it, he could simply start tossing flaming cannonballs into our bluebell fields. He's already done worse to the poor rock fauns."

Nettle really didn't know what she could possibly say. She wasn't sure how Piper could have known about Brawn. Maybe

Piper had followed her into the woods one day? Perhaps the voros moths told Piper things? Nettle knew he was a mistake from the start, but mistakes are sometimes the hardest things to put a stop to. She took Piper's trembling hands into her own. "Does anyone else know what you know?"

Piper wiped tears from her reddening eyes. "Not that I'm aware of."

"Will you promise me you'll keep it a secret?"

"If you promise to end it."

Piper. The life vein cocoon. Brawn. Nettle wasn't certain which of them were about to come to an end, but she was certain an end was coming.

Brawn did not like the cold, but there he was, standing in the middle of a dead, frozen grove just outside of his den. Nettle fluttered quietly through the woods and spied on him from between two aged oak trees. The satyr was making some gestures with his hands, as though performing a retelling of a wild story to an audience of nothing more than icy trees and scattered piles of long-cracked acorns.

She observed the spoiled prince a few moments longer, unsure of where exactly her heart might land.

"Watch this now, Nettle," he spoke suddenly, as if knowing she'd been there all along. Still without turning toward her, and with much concentration, Brawn waved a hand and stretched a couple of stubby fingers to their limits. An ethereal, shining blue vortex was conjured in front of him. It spiraled slowly and singed the freezing air for a moment before evaporating altogether.

Brawn looked at Nettle and smiled; he smiled not at her, but merely for himself. "Did you see?"

"Your magicks are getting better, Brawn. Though still altogether ineffectual."

He waved his arm in her direction. "Hmph. Trust *you* to crap on me with your faerie honesty."

Faerie honesty. Nettle was unsure if his comment was meant in jest of all of her secrets.

From across the icy grove, on a tree branch high above them, Nettle spotted the distinctive feather pattern of a rainbow-crested flitter. It was chirping to itself, but Nettle was certain its singsong contained words of sorrow and warnings.

They moved inside his tree home, not for the reasons Brawn had suspected they might. Completely the opposite, really. But Nettle still found ways to delay the inevitable. He sat himself upon his monstrous, blackened branch throne. She had never once asked about his peculiar throne, and chose that moment to do so.

"There once stood a tree five times as large as everything else around here. You could see it clearly from my father's home. From the window of his castle upon Tower Mountain. It used to be vibrant—green in the spring, golden in the summer. It smelled like everything I knew I ever wanted, and also like everything I ever lost." Absent-mindedly, Brawn picked at the charred bark of the throne, but then dusted it with the heel of his hand. Almost like an act of forgiveness. "Those things I lost regrettably, and the things I lost from my own doing. And then it burned. From the dirt of Sceanth to the blasted moon up there; it burned for months until this was all that remained." He tapped upon the seat with his meaty hand, then reached for his goblet—already full—and took a swig.

Nettle asked, "What caused the fire that killed this beautiful thing?"

He wiped his mouth with the sleeve of his dusty coat. "It was me."

The faerie's mouth straightened. It took her a minute longer to show any further reaction towards Brawn's terrible claims, though finally, Nettle blinked and asked, "Do you regret destroying the thing you once loved?"

Brawn smiled a smirk that indicated the answer was far too obvious. "What was it you came here to tell me, bluebell faerie?"

The flitter's song could be heard clearly from inside; loud, as though the bird had flown into Brawn's home. "I came to end this." The flitter sang happily then, and Nettle could not help hearing Piper's honey sweet voice from within it.

Brawn leaned in closer to her and asked, "Why do you not fear things, Nettle?"

Seemingly from nowhere, a thick fog that smelled of the sea crept into the satyr's den.

CHAPTER
9

TALEM HAD BEEN LEADING THE GIRLS THROUGH TWISTED, uneven tunnels for so long, the dried-out walls smelled nothing of the sea. This was not the way Kole and Nettle had traveled when they first sought Eamonn; this was a different route, one seemingly preferred by the chicken with no head.

Eventually, they emerged from the riven trunk of a dead tree, in the middle of some long-forgotten, dusty woods. Nettle did not know how far away these woods were from the fishing village; strangely, she had no sense at all of the ocean from here. This part of Erw seemed bereft of life. Dead snakes, squirrels, and spiders surrounded them; the remains of a deer deteriorated beside a log. The sour, stinging stink of death was inescapable. There were strange, black leaves covering the forest floor; odd-shaped leaves that resembled hands, fingers splayed. In every direction the girls turned, the ever-present sea smoke continued to hinder their view. Talem did not care about lingering death and decomposing carcasses, however, and continued along his inexplicable trajectory.

"How does a headless chicken know where it's going?" Kole asked, obviously frustrated by their apparent lack of direction. "Are we fools to follow this creature?" She lashed out at the side of a rotted tree with her forearm. A slab of dead bark fell to the sticky dirt.

"I trust in the bird," Nettle assured her. "Though there are obviously magicks at play here, I sense intent in his movement." Nettle walked carefully, a few steps ahead of Kole. She tried to avoid sniffing at the dead air around her. "But this place—I do not like being here."

Kole asked, "I don't like it either. These woods…these are not any woods I've ever seen." Crouching, Kole took one of the unusual black leaves into her hand, but released it almost immediately, like its very texture offended her. "Nettle, I'm not sure *where* we are."

Extending a hand, Nettle grasped at the sea smoke surrounding her. It was so thick her fingertips partially disappeared into its gray nothingness. "Just as I entered a different world when I came to Erw, perhaps we've now *both* entered another world? These dead woods…perhaps it is a place which defies the rules of your own home."

"Maybe we're *both* dreaming?"

Nettle knew her sudden silence was all-too obvious. She hoped another dream world was not the case here. Her fingers teased the sea smoke once again. "Is there truth in what Eamonn said? Is there truly some sort of witch who controls this miasma?"

"The only witches I've known exist in story books. But around here, there's a very fine line between bedtime stories, fairy tales, rumors, and the truth. The reality is, most people in Erw are content with not knowing any more than that. It's all a matter of what one wants."

It seemed selfish to Nettle. But it also seemed simple, which was likely the point Kole was trying to make. "What I want, I think, is to return to the ocean. But I am also afraid of it. Of what else it might be hiding." The faerie brought her hand back in; the sea smoke lingered, swirling around her sharp fingers like ethereal rings. "Is it normal, Kole? To fear the things you want?"

Kole did not answer; perhaps she simply did not know. But eventually she asked a question of her own. "Do witches exist in your world, Nettle? In Sceanth?"

"We have different names for such creatures. The bluebell faeries know them as root spirits. Past the Tower Mountains, they call them the gray women. Certain undines have been known to cast such dark spells, also. Yes, I've heard of them. Though I've not seen one."

There was a loud crack from somewhere unseen. Like the sound of something moving. Something approaching. Or something escaping. "Maybe we should just follow the bird and try to ignore these thoughts of other things," Kole suggested, wiping something from her eye.

"That way," Nettle said, sensing where Talem was at. They both ran ahead to catch up with the bird.

They crossed into a clearing that had small piles of broken stones on either side. Broken in half, as if something with the monstrous strength of a great beast was snapping the stones apart, looking for some hidden treasure inside them. The trees in the near distance were gray and bent and their branches' silhouettes appeared as clawed hands, reaching out like hungry specters.

Talem stopped at the edge of the clearing; he stood still, *buk-bawking* silently, perhaps on the precipice of making his next move.

"What is the bird doing?" Kole asked in a whisper.

"I cannot read his mind. He has no head." The faerie began making a move toward the chicken, in the hopes that a physical connection, a palm upon its feathers, might help explain its intentions. But Kole placed a hand of her own on Nettle's arm to hold her in place.

"Wait." Kole's hand was trembling. She was definitely sensing a presence in the dead woods. "Do you hear that?"

"I do." Directing her pointed ears all around them, Nettle

could make out the presence of *something*. A blowing wind, a rustling of dead things, a faraway voice. To Nettle, it was little more than a whisper, too quiet to make out the words. But there were definitely voices in the woods. "I've been hearing them since my arrival on Erw, but they've mostly been calling me in the other direction. Towards the ocean."

Talem remained at the clearing's edge, as still as taxidermy. Even through the sea smoke, Nettle could make out spider threads dangling from above, passing through the space where the bird's head would have been. Kole's grip tightened on Nettle's arm. Her eyes darted around, trying to pinpoint what it was she was hearing, and where she was hearing it. The cacophony in the air was obviously more unpalatable for Kole than it was for Nettle. The faerie moved a step, but Kole pulled her back. And even though there was no visible moon or stars to cast light from above, Nettle could see the sparkle of tears in the girl's eyes. "I—I'm scared, Nettle."

"Kole, the pain will pass," she told her, even though Nettle was not so confident in her own statement. A flickering glow of some instinct inside her told Nettle their path followed that of the chicken's. But she was also aware of burgeoning thoughts and feelings toward the girl, Kole. Inexplicably, she was fascinated by her. Like Kole had a glamour of her own. "I will keep you from harm."

Kole's palms were clammy. "I've been trying to keep things together. Ever since my family disappeared. First my father, then my mother after him. They raised me to be strong. But it's hard for me to admit how difficult things can be at times."

"Kole, do not burden yourself with things out of your control. The past has come and gone. It is unchangeable."

"The past—? They're still *gone*, Nettle. I'm still alone. But can you even understand? Do you even have a family of your own?"

In the lands of Sceanth, it was customary for bluebell faeries entering their second cycle to say farewell to their forebears before entering life vein cocoons, partly because life vein cocoons were often either stolen by huntsmen out for rewards or consumed by hungry critters feeding off faerie essence. Nettle's mother, however, chose to remain in the bluebell fields for reasons of her own. "I have not seen my own father for a very long time. And my mother and I did not speak often. Still, I realize the solace of bluebell traditions is no comfort for your own loss."

Kole's shaking hand touched the faerie's glowing cheek. "And whether I am meant to blame the ocean or this witch for the disappearance of my family, there's no solace in the fact that I'm still lonely."

Contrary to what Brawn thought, Nettle did have fears of her own. And they were only exacerbated in this dark realm she didn't know if she'd ever wake from. But she also could not bring herself to put her own worries over others, not when this girl was suffering, too. "I could very easily tell you to not be scared or lonely right now, Kole. But just know we are allowed to feel the ways others will tell us not to."

Removing her hand from Nettle's face, Kole sat back to consider a thousand things. It was obvious she was becoming drawn into the faerie's beguiling details: how her glow lit the murkiness surrounding her in a faint amber-pink, the way her eyes' iridescence shifted and swirled like the alluring sheen upon soap bubbles, the juxtaposition between her dark lilac hair and the gentle light within her. The creature before Kole was like nothing she knew, and, although she did not wish to deny the existence of the faerie's so-called glamour, she felt there were some other feelings at play. With half a smile, she said, "I didn't imagine any of this happening when I woke up this morning."

"And upon entering my life vein cocoon for the last time, I did not know to expect this world, or tales of serpents and witches and mystic trees. Or that chicken over there." Nettle turned back to Talem, still unmoving. And without returning her eyes to Kole, she added, "Or you."

Kole only pursed her lips at this.

Looking back at Kole, Nettle finally said, "I saw one. An Obsidian Revenant."

"You saw——? Where?"

She ran sharp fingertips through her lilac hair, as if combing the thoughts from her memory. "On the island. Last night. When I flew over the ocean's crashing waves, the small, wooded island appeared, and I thought at first it was a shadowy figure. It was really a massive, black tree on the island's precipice." Nettle's hair was already taking on a darker shade, as though adopting sinister properties of Erw itself.

"There's no island out there."

"Surely you've seen enough in your life to make you question the things you thought you might've known?"

Kole's pauses and hesitations seemed to be getting longer. "You told me there was a cave, didn't you? You entered a cave and were attacked by something. Or someone. And then you woke up on the beach."

"And then you found me." Nettle blinked. To Kole, it felt like slow motion.

"And then I found you," Kole said, swallowing hard.

"But it *was* an island I found out there. It was a *tree* I entered. And it was the Obsidian Revenant, I'm certain of it." Nettle recalled the pain she felt when Eamonn showed her the shard from the great tree. Even without physical contact, it was like daggers stabbing at her body. And when she was inside the Obsidian, how she felt her power begin to fade. How its pitch-blackness overwhelmed her. Whatever power the nebulous darkness had over the faerie's light, it was substantial. Nettle quivered thinking about it again.

"If you've seen it, that means you can find it. So why are we following this chicken?"

"My feelings are...scattered. And uncertain." Nettle stopped. She closed her eyes to concentrate on what was around her. Though there remained far-off voices in the woods, there was another noise within the wind, and it wasn't coming from the ocean. Within the sound there were many components, and Nettle tried to disseminate each one: a static fuzz, a flapping of dragonfly wings like the rustling of worn paper, soft nutshells cracking, water trickling, the hustle and bustle of cities she re-called visiting while inside her life vein cocoon. She breathed in deep and picked up a mix of scents: from the familiar fields of bluebells, to the wonderfully transient moments in her dreams, to the still-lingering saltwater of this world's strange, sentient ocean. She also sensed Kole; the girl's strengths, her fears, and her loneliness were all forming a curious black glow drawing her nearer.

And then—before Nettle knew what was really happening, before her senses returned to her—she felt lips upon her own.

If this truly was a dream, it was suddenly not as terrible as it first seemed.

Their lips parted. Nettle opened her eyes and Kole was there, a jittery, tremulous look about her. "I'm sorry, Nettle. I just… it's just that—"

Shaking her head clear, Nettle dismissed her with a hand. "It's like I said to you earlier: it is merely the glamour. But it's fine, Kole. Stronger minds than yours have been weakened by the abilities of fae." Without another word or concern, the faerie extended her wings and fluttered across the clearing. She wanted to say more, to loosen some of the uncertainty within her, but instead chose to say nothing.

Kole walked after her. "Nettle, I'm sorry. I am. Whether this is the glamour or not, I—"

"There is no need for apologies," Nettle spoke, perhaps cutting off Kole's words quicker than she meant to. The faerie tried to discern some detail from within the dark smoke surrounding them. "At least not for me."

"For who, then?"

"For Eamonn. It seems as though we've lost his chicken."

CHAPTER
10

A SCREAMING WIND BLEW THROUGH THE DEAD WOODS. It scratched their bodies as it passed; Nettle felt its harshness lash her bare arms while it seemed to claw at Kole's skin, even through her thick sweater. The night was quickly melding into day, yet Erw's sun had yet to shine. There was still no sign of Eamonn's headless chicken, either. Kole questioned whether Talem would be able to find his way back again, since the seeking of magick trees seemed to be his only purpose. *Destiny*, she recalled what Eamonn had called it. But Nettle was more in favor of trusting Talem's abilities. Almost like a kindred spirit.

As they navigated through the darkness without direction, Nettle shared her dreams. Eyes wide, Kole listened, while also finding it difficult to not entwine her fingers within the faerie's glow permeating the space alongside her. There was something about the glow that helped to keep Kole's cracked, calloused, and weather-worn hands from freezing entirely. To help relieve their unrest, Kole spoke of her own dreams, which were mostly of warm homes and freshly baked bread. Her family had already begun to seep from her dreams, taking space in her memories alone.

Kole walked ahead. Her boots ceased squelching in the mud as the ground became drier and drier. On and off cackles and howls of unseen hauntings and spirits faded, eventually becoming nothing more than insect chirps, frog croaks, and the distant calls of nightbirds.

Nettle told Kole about her life on Sceanth. About her relationships with Piper, with Brawn, and others. How they began and how they ended. "Brawn was seething as I flew away from him for the last time," she said. "But I did not turn around. I went right back to the bluebell fields. I spoke briefly with my mother, but soon realized I needed the comfort of my life vein cocoon instead. If only for a little bit, I needed to dream. Upon waking, I planned to end things with Piper, too. I just didn't know how I might say the words. Maybe I would find them in my dreams? But I dreamed of the dead. And of screams. And then, instead of waking up back in Sceanth with a mind set on hurting Piper, I woke up *here*."

Kole peered back at her, over her shoulder. "And that is why you're not sure if you wish to return to your world?" She stopped momentarily and inspected an innocuous tree with both palms.

"Maybe. Maybe it's just easier this way. Being here. But this world frightens me too. Well"—she continued, slowly breaking her gaze from Kole—"not *all* of it." Kole smiled, though Nettle had already turned away, towards the tops of the trees.

As she looked up, Nettle spotted the shapes of two birds circling the trees above them. She could hear their feathers scraping against the wind. Kole saw them too. Ravens, they both believed.

One of black and one of white.

Kole snuck a long glance as Nettle was still looking up. The otherworldly glowing creature captured her attention. And also her sense of wonder. "So, you've been with faeries *and* goat people?"

"Satyrs, they're called."

"That's…odd. I've not been in a single relationship."

"Not one?"

"Nothing like yours. Nothing so great, nor anything so terrible. That's for certain. And if there was something that fell in between the two, I doubt I even noticed. In my village, we don't have much time for matters of the heart. It's all work and worry, hoping the ocean doesn't come and take everything away." Kole looked up again, though what it was she was looking for, if it was anything at all, was unclear. "I guess it still did in the end."

Allowing Nettle to come closer, Kole reached her hand out again, into the comfort of the faerie's glow. Nettle placed her own hand into Kole's. "The end still has yet to happen, Kole." Their hands squeezed together, and Nettle felt a sudden, indiscernible presence, like there was something between their palms that wasn't there a moment ago. She let go and looked into her hand to be sure, but there was nothing there.

Studying her own palm, Kole said, "Unless there is not meant to be an end." Nettle tilted her head inquisitively as Kole continued. "I've read fairy tales in which beginnings and ends do not exist. Life and death and everything else within them are only cycles, meant to go around and around."

Nettle thought about this. "If there is no end, then what are we left with?"

"*Hope*, of course. It's why we have the great serpent. All we have is hope, Nettle."

The faerie turned to face the forest canopy. The ravens were gone. "In *my* world, hope is more like tidings. We will wish for them, good and bad, tying cloths to the clootie trees in order to manifest our hope. And the tidings, they will come and go as the moon's phases do." She turned back to Kole, who had yet another incomprehensible look on her face. "I am sorry. I realize some of what happens on Sceanth must seem peculiar to you. Perhaps too far-reaching?"

"No"—Kole started—"well, yes. But I can't help from also finding it all very…fascinating." Nettle fluttered a little off their rudimentary path. There was a shift in the air around them, and she placed a hand on some berry bushes in order to gain a sense of what it could be. Kole watched her every move. She asked, "Are there differences? Between faeries and satyrs? I mean, what's better?"

"Better—? It's not really about better or worse. There are differences, but bluebell faeries don't really notice them. We do not see things the same way as you might."

"Believe me, Nettle. I see things a bit differently than most around here."

Nettle bit her lower lip as a memory passed through her mind. She said, "Some faeries do *kiss* like satyrs, I can tell you that much." Playfully, she stuck out her ruby tongue in disgust. The two of them actually snickered at the same time, and they both blushed; Kole's face reddened while Nettle's aura momentarily burned a darker red.

Kole paused. "My grandfather once told me a story about an encounter he had at sea. He was fishing, just himself out there on the water. But the sea smoke moved in, and his boat capsized; the ocean again, taking whatever it liked. He told me an angel had come. Her wings lit her way through the mist. She saved him from Erw's volatile ocean and flew my grandfather back to shore where she restored his strength with a kiss."

"And did it work?"

Kole smiled a selfish sort of smile, recollecting the story but knowing there was more to it. "It did. He woke up and saw her face, her lips still upon his. He was saved. And yet—"

"Yes—?"

"He told me she kissed like a horse with a fish in its mouth." She laughed, adding, "But I think he only said that because my grandmother always hated him telling the angel story."

Nettle laughed along a little with Kole, though she was uncertain if she understood the details correctly. A light rain began tapping upon the foliage above them.

"I don't know if I ever fully believed his story. But now I'm wondering if maybe he wasn't visited by a bluebell faerie himself."

"So, you are saying I kiss like a horse with a fish mouth?"

Nettle asked, remembering Kole's lips earlier in the dead woods.

"That is *not* what I'm saying, Nettle! I'm just thinking that maybe the things I didn't believe in before were actually something else instead. And perhaps not so impossible." Kole stopped and leaned against a tree, its vitality was clear from the damp moss and dewy spiderwebs covering it. "My grandfather wished for me to one day see an angel, too. That's what he told me. But my own father forbade me from going out onto the water. Told me it was no place for his daughter."

Nettle's disposition tempered immediately. "I do not allow men to make decisions for me. Or tell me what it is I can or cannot do."

"You don't understand my father," Kole spoke solemnly. "Or his demons. Or my reasons for wanting him back."

"I too have experienced grief with my own father." The memory of her father pained Nettle a little. Just thinking about him. "I do not presume to know how things work here, Kole. I've only been in this land for a short time. But my father… he was not true. And the other men I've known, well…though bluebell faeries and the denizens of Sceanth do not perceive relationships the same way as the people of Erw might, I have certainly been soured on pursuing further relationships with men." The faerie bit her lip even harder, until the skin purpled. But Kole did not speak; she was waiting for Nettle to say something more. With a mischievous smirk, like that of an imp, Nettle said, "Did you know satyrs have incessant erections?"

Nearly choking on a surprise laugh, Kole said, "Oh my. Now *that* has got to be embarrassing."

"Oh, Brawn was not embarrassed at all. He proudly walked around with it."

"Oh, Gods. I cannot imagine that at all," Kole said. "I don't know how or why you put up with him. It sounds like he was not very good for you."

Nettled sighed. The satyr's flimsy promises of buried oceans echoed in her memory. "Bluebells are all about change. Without it, we are not really bluebells. But we never know if the change is worth it until it's already been done."

"Change is not just for bluebell faeries, Nettle. It's *everyone*. It's natural." Kole stepped around a tree and peeled back a wall of lush ferns behind it. She peered at Nettle from the corner of an eye, then waved for her to follow. "This whole land is about hope for change, really. Come see."

It had not gone unnoticed by Nettle that Kole had been leading the way. "Where is it we're going, anyway?"

Kole ignored the faerie's query in favor of one of her own. "Are you still tracking the chicken?"

"I lost Talem's energy long ago."

"Then, I suppose you should be grateful you've had someone else to follow." She passed through the veil of ferns, calling back behind her. "Just another few steps, Nettle. We're nearly there."

Trading steps for flight, Nettle released her wings and fluttered past the foliage over to where Kole was headed. There was a large standing stone in the middle of a clearing; the woods around them had grown decidedly less dead than where they had been just a short distance back. Life was resurfacing. Dried dirt became muddier. Ferns more green than gray curled and unfurled. Bugs crept and crawled along mossy stones and tree branches, finding more and more sustenance. Most notably, the far-off screams lessened, being replaced slowly with a cool wind whistling along the girls' cheeks and past their ears, carrying the ocean's scent. A light rain misted the air, but the cold, wet forest was still preferable over where they'd journeyed through.

The standing stone was carved into some intentional, and oddly familiar, shape. What had first appeared to be a pointed, spiralling design, Nettle soon recognized as a larger-scale version of the one she had seen earlier in the village—the copper idol that sat upon Kole's mantle. It was easily twice as large as either of the girls. "This is the serpent shrine," Kole explained to Nettle, and the faerie immediately recalled its existence from both Kole and Eamonn having mentioned it. This is where the village would come to pay homage or pray to the great serpent. Littering the base of the altar were a collection of animalistic, tooth-and-claw scratch marks.

In this clearing, there was no sea smoke at all. Not a wisp of it. All around there were healthy green and brown saplings reaching up, stretching towards the light cracking through the canopy above.

Kole said softly, "At first I didn't know where we were going, like I was lost in my own land. But I could sense when we were getting closer to it."

Nettle's eyes glowed a little brighter. "Like a beacon of hope. There certainly is an energy here." Nettle waved a finger through the misty air and brought it to her mouth, licking her fingertip. It tasted of magick, of iron and storms and a crackling, invisible energy. Though not like anything she knew from Sceanth, and not exactly like anything she'd so far discovered in Erw. This was a different kind of power. But whether it fell into a feeling of wonder or that of fear, or somewhere in between, she was unsure. She placed a firm hand upon the carved stone and turned back to Kole, who had stepped closer to her than she realized. "Who built it?"

"Some men from my village. My grandfather helped."

"Your grandfather? The one who met the angel?"

"The same." Kole crouched and braced herself with a hand on the forest floor. "One morning he left our village. He came here to the serpent shrine, but he never returned." If there were ghosts of family haunting this stone, Kole couldn't sense them. A part of her always hoped she might be given the opportunity to find her grandfather again, if only she kept returning to this place.

But there was no sense of anything at all.

"Perhaps he found his angel again?"

Kole's eyes were wet and sad. "Perhaps."

Nettle placed a warm, glowing hand on Kole's shoulder. "Have we come here to find hope?"

Kole touched the faerie's hand on her shoulder with her

own. "Or maybe just to wish for good tidings? Do you want to return to Sceanth, Nettle? What if you could be with Piper again? Without ever having been in that mess with Brawn. What if you could see your father once more?"

The solid stone serpent loomed large before them. Even carved in rock, its eyes appeared benign, its teeth merciful. Nettle was full of questions. "Is that really how it works?"

"To be honest, I don't know how any of it works. I come here to pray."

"Pray? For what?"

"A gift, maybe. But I'm not sure if it matters, really." Kole crouched in front of the shrine. Her knees touched the scratch marks at its base. "Do you know what it is *you* might want?"

"I'm not sure if that matters either," Nettle said with an ephemeral smirk. She kneeled next to Kole and closed her eyes just as the fisher girl did, and considered all she knew about gifts.

CHAPTER
11

When her father requested her company for his walk to Thistlemoor on that day, Nettle was uncertain. He made the trek once every half-moon, in order to trade faerie offerings—potables, baubles, and other curiosities—for Snippet eggs and vegetables that grew in the more fertile dirt of Thistlemoor. He would always walk alone. And he would always *walk*, claiming the route's terrain to be the most pleasurable path for one's feet. Nettle was still young, her wings had not yet grown enough to fly. Still, she could not understand why a faerie would choose to step amongst the pernicious glimmer giants, satyrs, and even humans, when they could instead soar above them.

But Nettle had a teaching today, and the other young bluebells were gathering to listen to Agatha, an elder fae who taught them of the world and of the bluebell ways from beneath the sacred white alder tree. Nettle's father waved her concerns of teachings away with a limp-wristed hand, claiming he had missed a countless number of Agatha's teachings in his own youth, and was no worse for it. "Now come, daughter. These hands of mine could use the help of yours. You're never too young to start choosing paths."

Nettle's father was a smallish fae, but he preferred keeping himself unnoticed; rarely gesticulating and maintaining a speech of a low, insignificant tone. He had a dark, unkempt beard, a wild mop of hair atop his head, a foul grimace, and an intense look in his eyes. His dim glow was a sickly, yellowish-brown.

It was some time after they passed the juni spring when Nettle noticed something behind them dart into a cluster of tall ferns. Whatever it was she'd seen, it had reflected the sun's sparkle off its glittering hide. She tugged on her father's long linen shirt hoping he might have seen the creature too, but he had not. "Let's see if I can't find it for you, though," her father said. He was notorious for being able to find almost anything; if a bluebell faerie lost a leaf in a storm, he would promise to find it, and nearly always did. Spreading the ferns apart, Nettle's father took a quick peek, then stepped through, the ferns flopping back into their place.

Nettle waited for him in the silence of the forest. From where she stood, she could see the spire of the giant golden tree in the distance, five times as large as any others in its vicinity. It was a beautiful tree: a wondrous emerald green in the spring and Nettle knew well of its golden shine in the summer.

"Father—?" she called out, curious as to what had been taking him such a time. She could hear not the rustling of leaves or the padding of bare feet over twigs and dirt. "Father?" Nettle breached the ferns herself and stepped into a wide clearing with no sign of her father or whatever creature he was after.

"Father, are you—"

Gone. He was unmistakably, unequivocally gone.

Nettle tried to press on, but she soon came to realize she was unsure of where the farms of Thistlemoor and their Snippet eggs might be exactly. So, she eventually turned around and followed a voros moth along the path back to the faerie hills and bluebell fields.

When she returned home, her mother and father were both

there. They had been worried about her and were wondering where it was she'd disappeared to. Fairly confused, Nettle explained the afternoon as it had happened, but her father had no recollection and claimed he'd never left the bluebell fields.

The next day, beneath the sacred, milk-white alder, young bluebell fae had gathered for a teaching with Agatha. The wise faerie had finished an earlier lesson on linen dyeing, and the tying of the brightly-colored cloths to nearby clootie trees for good tidings. The children's hands and faces were still kaleidoscopes of dyes made from roots, berries, and lichen. Nettle's face was bright green while Clementine, Sprig, and Flora were all thoroughly chaotic patchworks of color. The young, gangly Piper was still spotless, after not wishing to participate in the messy activity.

The elder Agatha was well-respected amongst all the bluebell faeries, and she was as beautiful as she was judicious. In fact, her beauty was almost mystifying in its perfection: the exquisite point her nose and chin were pulled towards, her cheekbones were as pronounced as her great dimples were hollowed, her earth-brown eyes were as wide and alert as a deer's, and her silky hair framed her face like the curved leaves of a hazelnut. She wore a crystalline indigo gimcrack around her neck (its origin was ever an enigma, she would half-explain with a wink). She had inkings on her arms: a killorn tree branch on one and a whistling farrow on the other. The only parts of Agatha's beauty that were ever questioned were her oddly rounded ears.

Sometimes the children would ask the reasons for why her ears were not pointed like all bluebell faeries. But Agatha would not say. There was never a mention of an enigma or an accompanying wink.

She had just settled the children down with a discussion about faerie gifts. "Every generation," she said with honey sweet candor, "another fae will be tasked with gifting a human.

Some, *more* than once. It is unavoidable. It is inevitable. And it might even be one of *you*, my bluebells."

"What kind of gift?" the always-inquisitive Clementine asked.

"A gift can be many a different thing. Something as simple as love—for love really is quite simple. Or it could be granting your faerie magicks to a human. Even having or giving a human baby."

Some of the children's eyes rolled at the idea of babies. "Yuck," Sprig gagged loudly.

Nettle asked, "Are we not taught to avoid humans?"

"Some, we certainly must eschew. But some are not so terrible. And even some others are much like us, really." Agatha's large eyes wandered up the white alder tree, into its cluster of shimmering leaves. "But those humans are not found on Sceanth. They are the ones you will only find by crossing into their worlds."

Again, Clementine was ready with another question. "How do fae cross into human worlds?"

"Through spells. Bluebell magicks. Life vein cocoons." She looked carefully at each of the children. "You will all have your own life vein cocoon eventually. It is bluebell tradition. They are the beginning of your next stage."

Sprig commented, "I've heard of what happens in the next stage. Yuck!"

Some of the children giggled, while Nettle wondered: "But they sound dangerous, these cocoons. Are they dangerous?"

"Only if you choose your life veins poorly," Agatha said.

"How do we learn to choose?"

"No one can teach you. That is up to *you*, Nettle. But when the air is sticky like spider webs and it tastes of cinnamon and frost, you will enter your second phase. And this is when you will begin to discover who you *really* are. Who you will be. And how you will choose your life veins." She took a moment to settle Sprig and a few of the others back down.

"And what of the tithes?" Piper asked amidst the ebbing commotion.

"What do you know of tithes, Piper?"

"I've heard that to give a gift means to also pay a tithe. You have to *kill* something. Or someone."

Kill. A couple of the children stopped at the word, as it was a word that was not used openly in the bluebell fields.

Agatha did not wish the mood to become tenebrous. "It is not always a life which the tithe demands. It is sometimes an unwanted transformation, or an exile. Of sorts." The kind elder fae took a moment before continuing, adjusting the bright red strings tied around her wrists. "I was once tasked with gifting a human." She smiled a wistful smile, remembering. "He was wonderful. He truly was."

"But then you must also have been tasked with taking a life?" Clem asked.

The smile across her lips did not quiver or break. Not at all. "I was. And I did." Agatha shook the thoughts from her mind. "But that is a story for another time, my bluebells. When you are all much, much older. And—hopefully—as wise as I once was."

Months passed. Nettle noticed her father changing in small ways; his treks to Thistlemoor and other distant hamlets had him away for longer periods than he used to be. He trimmed his beard and was combing his hair. Strangest of all, he spoke a lot about oceans. Of their bitter coldness and of their salty essence that clung to the air. But mostly of their infinite beauty. He'd never spoken about oceans before.

And one day, Nettle returned to the bluebell fields to find her mother tying yet more cloths to their own clootie tree. There was a sacred well within the faerie enchantment that she used for dyeing the fabric. Nettle questioned her mother's reasons for this sudden plea for good fortune.

"Your father has been with a human," Cleo said bluntly. "He got caught up in their tricks, and has found his way into their world, and back again."

"He has been gone for some time now," Nettle noted. She couldn't pinpoint when exactly she'd last seen her father.

"Oh, he returns from time to time to tell me of his escapades. He's gifted one of them, too. With *love*. Love! The fool. And as such, he has returned to the human world to complete his tithe."

"A tithe?" Nettle had to take a moment to process the news, recalling all Agatha had taught her about gifts and tithes. And the simplicity of love.

"And he may not return, daughter. Have I not taught you the dangers of humans and their trickster ways? Of the darkness they bring to all creatures, but especially to bluebell faeries?"

"You have, Mother. But you need not warn *me*. Perhaps it was *him* who needed to hear your words?"

"Perhaps." Cleo was quick to dismiss whatever thoughts were still bubbling within her, and she went back to tying cloths to the tree.

Nettle was reminded of her mother's warnings, of which she always took seriously. It was not uncommon for Cleo to go on about it at the mealing table. But her father had a way of smirking to himself when Cleo mentioned the humans. He rolled his eyes. Nothing daunted him it seemed; fear was not a concern of his. A growling, unseen creature beneath a shaking bush would not be enough to scare him away, as evidenced by the day months before: the day Nettle was still certain her father had first disappeared. Where he should have been fearful of humans like all bluebells, instead, all indications were that Nettle's father quite likely wished—even dared—to meet one.

Still, she remained more than a little uncertain of how these tithes really worked. If her mother hinted at an exile of sorts— or something worse, something far, far worse—she did not know. And she did not know if her father might return again, or if he was truly lost to the bluebell faeries and all he'd left behind in Sceanth.

With the memories now fresh in her mind, Nettle opened her iridescent eyes cautiously. She was no longer beneath the sacred alder or at the clootie tree. Nor was she waking in a strange bed or beneath it. She was not at the shore of the fishing village, and she was not in an underwater cave in the body of a mermaid. Nettle was back in the clearing, her knees still resting upon the serpent shrine.

Kole continued to pray beside her.

To be certain of her place, the faerie felt the ground with her palms then stood, her light frame still heavy enough to crush branches beneath her. She glanced back down and wriggled her bare toes in the moist dirt, smiling at the intimacy of it.

And Nettle was caught by surprise when Kole asked, "Are you okay, Nettle?"

"I…I had memories just now."

"Were they good ones?"

"Some. I believe." The faerie extended her wings and hovered above the ground. All of a sudden, she was not sure if Erw enjoyed the feeling of her feet upon it. "Were you praying, Kole? For a gift?"

Kole nodded, perhaps apprehensively. "It was more than that, though. Like a vision. It felt like a memory…familiar, but not." She hesitated, eyes watering. Something shuffled in the branches above. "I saw my family. One moment I was right here—with *you*—then I opened my eyes, and I was on a boat. We were fishing, my father and grandfather and me." Kole looked upwards, inspecting the noise in the treetops. Nettle did not turn to look. "I'd told you, hadn't I? How my father never wished for me to be out on the water? And it was terrifying, actually. The waves pounded the boat. The ocean was hungry for us. I lowered the trawling net and caught something. Some…*creature* that had no right being caught. There was a murky glow in the water. But then our boat was attacked—by the ocean, or some other force?—and we lost it. It got away, whatever it was. I knew, somehow, it was only the hint of something I would forever strive to see again." Another twisted branch shook above them, creaking. A few brown leaves floated down to their feet. "It was only a dream though, wasn't it?"

Nettle nodded the faintest of nods. The faerie sat herself upon a tree stump on the edge of the clearing. She was hoping an insect might crawl onto her fingers—to tickle her just enough to know for sure she was alive—but there were no bugs about. She retracted her wings in order to limit the amount of her that was exposed to this place. "I've been thinking…of my life vein cocoon. And how I came to choose this place."

"You mentioned your cocoon before. I'm still not really sure what it means. Is it like that of an insect's? Like a butterfly?"

Nettle tried to smile. "Not really, no." She fought through hesitation and finally stepped back over to Kole's side. "A butterfly's place will already be decided upon the caterpillar entering its cocoon. Bluebell faeries do not know what is in store for them. It all depends on the dreams inside the cocoon. Which life veins they follow. Some will wake with purpose. Some may still be lost."

Kole looked past Nettle, out somewhere beyond the shrine. She said, "I am, too. Like the great serpent, I am also lost."

Nettle's eyes flared. "As am I," she spoke quietly. "Though being lost in another's world, no matter how dark, is somehow easier than being lost in your own." Carefully, Nettle touched Kole just under the ear, and traced a line along the serpent tattoo, until her sharp fingertip hooked onto the neck of the sweater. The girls locked eyes. There was most certainly a magick in their connection. Something brought from Sceanth and something found in Erw; drawn together by this world's strange sea smoke and wonderful dreams gone horribly awry. "I think I know…" The faerie's words trailed off.

"What is it—?"

The faerie continued, "I think I know now what it is I've come here for." Nettle thought of Piper—her love of river stones and her laughter like honey—and if she might ever see her again. "I have a *gift* for you, Kole."

She reached down and scratched some dirt from the ground. It was cold, perhaps slightly frozen from the lingering deadness permeating this land, but Nettle took the dirt into her hands and rubbed it onto her own forearms nevertheless. She gathered some of the leaves around her, too. As well as some tiny, splintered branches and bits of shattered nutshells and pressed them into her palms. Kole watched wide eyed and carefully, unsure of what was happening exactly.

Around them in the clearing was something between a glow and a shadow. Between alive and dead. Though neither girl noticed the world happening around them. Still with leaves and earth in her hands, Nettle brought her mouth to Kole's. The fisher girl's lips were cracked and dusty, with the lingering taste of ocean spray. Kole had momentarily stopped, something deep within her had wanted to hold back, but she eventually gave in.

Nettle opened her wings again; she stretched them as wide as possible. A glorious shiver shot up her spine. Both girls' feet lifted away; toes hovered inches above the ground. The forest floor undulated a little, as the beady eyes of a few curious dirt bugs burrowed to the surface. Stark white sprouts of burgeoning life poked up, too. The leaves in Nettle's grip flared a bright green. The amber-pink light seeping from the faerie's kiss caused the darkness to quake and shudder, and momentarily fade. There were also the shrill, startled caws of two distant birds above.

Nettle had visions of humans she did not know. Men calling to shore from boats cresting vicious waves. Another man, his beard scraggly, his eyes a certain glassy darkness about them.

Kole saw a wondrous green landscape, lush with life and sparkling river currents. The strange calls of birds she did not recognize. She saw the half-goat man, his hairy back turned to her, toying with blue magicks.

When their lips finally released, the surrounding woods of Erw blackened a little. It happened so fast the girls did not even notice a change at all.

Beads of sweat had formed on Kole's brow. Her dark gray eyes held a sparkle of amber not seen before. She felt weak, too, and had to seat herself on the ground. Her heart beat faster than she'd ever recalled.

Nettle shook her own head clear. "Kole? Are you—?"

"Give me a moment." Her world stopped spinning and she finally caught her breath. "What just happened there?"

The faerie did not move. Her eyes' iridescence shifted and flowed in strange patterns. "How do you feel?"

"I feel…feel like I need another drink."

"Something stronger than dew water, I suppose?"

"Definitely," Kole smiled slyly.

"And so—?"

They watched one another in perfect silence for a moment, hoping to comprehend but a fraction of what had just occurred between them.

"So. I know of a town not far from here. Let's go find something stronger."

The faerie took Kole's hand and helped her to her feet. She pulled a large branch aside and stepped past a felled tree, back into the forest once more. And they stumbled back into the woods, without letting go of one another.

CHAPTER
12

MANY TIMES, KOLE HAD SNUCK AWAY FROM THE VILLAGE, claiming her destination to be the shrine. But the shrine was actually not far from another village. A small town, really. Those who lived in the town of Yarari were not fisherfolk, for Yarari was not built on the oceanside. It sat safely upon the hilltops. Here, citizens made their livings from masonry and metalwork. Not all places that existed in Erw were fit to have names attached to them, and Yarari was not fit for much, but it did at least have a name to call its own.

Kole would visit Yarari in order to drink. There seemed to be too many taverns and alehouses for the local population alone, as though they had all been constructed with the empty hopes of serving visitors and passersby. Travelers who might venture through only because they were lost or sneaking away from somewhere else. Ale was cheap and its servers never questioned the patronage of children or youthful near-adults, and Kole would drink until she felt about as poorly and as numb as she could. Sometimes, before stumbling back to her own home,

Kole would even spoil herself and pay for a warm bath at a Yarari inn.

"You know this place well," Nettle noted as Kole led her through murky, labyrinthine alleyways with purpose. "I can sense familiarity in your eyes." The alleys reeked of something new: of filth and greasy food boiling somewhere behind stone walls and wafting out through open windows or cracks in the infrastructure.

"Well enough, I suppose. Though I've not been here for a while now." Kole breathed in the town's pungency. "I miss this place. Yarari just might be the one place I can go to forget my troubles."

"But forgetting troubles won't make them go away, Kole," the observant faerie said.

"Aye. But the drinking still helps."

From the dirt-pathed backstreets, the girls stepped onto a cobblestone road. Crooked two- and three-story buildings loomed over them, black and gothic. Like rows of hungry, dim-lit spirits. Iron gas lamps littered the streets, half of which were burned out. Nettle felt vulnerable in this place, scuttling like witless prey through the winding streets, where a myriad of windows might have held any number of shadow-veiled eyes. The girls continued to hold onto one another.

They came to a dingy, unmarked building with frosted glass windows, though the clinking of glasses and hollering of men inside were enough to know it was a tavern. A few barrels were stacked up outside, leaning like a passing breeze might cause them to tumble and roll down the road. The heavy door creaked as the girls entered. Nettle had never been to such a place. A putrid smell hit her instantly. The interior was lit by a few scattered oil lanterns for only a couple of men seated at one of the thick, round tables. Glasses littered the surface of the table, with some more having been knocked onto the wet floor. Glistening ale seeped in and around the cracks between floorboards like the ocean waves lapped the shore. There were more barrels in every corner.

Another man stood behind a counter, bottles and glasses of every size over his hunched shoulders and out of reach. Reflections from the lanterns lit their surfaces with tints of various liquors. The man was in the midst of counting some coins he'd emptied onto the countertop from a small cloth bag. The tiny clinking of tinny coins echoed the lost nature of Nettle's own soul. Kole walked over to the bar and Nettle reluctantly followed behind.

With shifty, assuming eyes, the barkeep watched them approach. He pulled his money in towards himself and grunted a hello.

Kole looked at the selection of bottles behind the barkeep and—almost like she knew exactly what she wanted—pointed at one in particular. "Two glasses, if you will." Nettle recalled Kole speaking of this place earlier; of this drink, too, and the girl's need for drinking it.

The man's eyes shot back and forth between the girls. "You from one of them fishing villages?" His voice was not nearly as gruff as they might have assumed, but the barkeep was still a long way away from soft pleasantries. "We don't like your kind around here." Across the room, the two drunken heads turned as the man's voice raised.

Pulling some coins of her own from a pocket, Kole plunked them on the counter and said, "But you'll take our money, nevertheless, won't you?"

The barkeep did not touch the money, nor did he answer, but turned and pulled the bottle in question from the shelf, filling two grimy glasses half-way. He gave each glass a push towards the girls, still eyeing them up. "Twins, is it?"

Kole appeared confused.

"Looks can be deceiving," Nettle answered, as she did when Kole first asked about her glamour.

"Hmph," he replied, and he put the lid back on the bottle before returning it to its place on the shelf. "And I won't take your coins, girl. I do not take the money of fools." With a sneer, he looked Nettle up and down; the barefoot girl in nothing but a thin, filthy dress. "And by the looks of *you*, girl, that money might be better spent on proper—" He stopped mid-thought, and suddenly could not unlock his eyes from Nettle. Though the barkeep did not know it, it was the glamour that had him seeing something else. Only momentarily, however, and he soon shook his head clean of faerie magick. With some confusion, he moved down to the other end of the bar to tidy up an earlier mess he'd only just realized had been left unattended.

Kole's eyes widened at this display of power.

Nettle sniffed at the contents in the glass and squirmed. It reminded her of the swill Brawn would guzzle from his worn goblet. She looked at the coins, still sitting where Kole had placed them. "What is it that makes him call us fools?"

Kole, still in awe of the faerie, gave her head a shake. "The people of Yarari look down upon those who live on the shores. Like we are lesser and more naïve for living so close to the thing that only wants to destroy us."

Though far away from the ocean now, Nettle could still pinpoint the tides and crashing waves from within the Yarari tavern's din.

Kole took a few gulps of her drink, relishing the strength of its bitter causticity.

Nettle said, "They have their secrets, and you have yours. I, too. But secrets cannot be weighed or measured." She thought of her clandestine relationship with the satyr prince and didn't have to dig very deep to know the words she spoke to Kole could not have been further from the truth. She dipped a fingertip into the drink; it felt sweet on her skin, while also throbbing like the sting of a day-old sliver. There was another feeling, too. It was difficult to put a label on it, but it was a feeling of *truth*. "What do you call this drink?" she asked.

"I'm not sure what's written on the bottle, but I call it Glory."

"And it is good?"

Kole smiled. "It is. The Glory is very, very good. Glory helps to forget the past and also to see the future." Nettle knew of some potent drinks on Sceanth, but nothing so capable of what Kole boasted. "Tell me another secret," Kole stammered. She nudged the other glass closer to Nettle, and almost slipped drunkenly from her seat in doing so. "Glory is also helpful for getting secrets out."

Nettle still did not know what force had led her to fall asleep inside her life vein cocoon only to wake up in the dark realm of Erw. She hoped she might see Piper again, though simultaneously, she wished she might not. She was unsure what might come from the kiss she shared with Kole at the serpent shrine. And she was beginning to fear her mother's last words about the dangers of entering other worlds. She breathed in deeply before taking a tiny sip of the drink. It was pungent, though not as terrible as she first presumed. Nettle's eyes tightened mischievously. "If it is out, then it is no longer a secret." She looked back at the few coins still on the counter, and said, "How about I *show* you something instead?"

Slowly, trance-like, and with a hand hovering above the coins, the faerie activated her flare. Before their eyes, the coins rattled slightly upon the wooden countertop and also went from having a dull luster to a sparkling, amber-pink shine. Kole and Nettle looked at one another and smiled. They touched hands beneath the counter, too; an invisible energy crackled between them.

The barkeep caught the coins' glare, also. With the sleeve of his dirtied shirt, he swiped the money from the counter, and they clinked and spun upon the floor. "I don't take the money of witches, either!" He shouted toward the door with a wave of his hand. "Out with you and your accursed spells!"

Kole turned to him, wobbly and a bit off-balance; her eyes alight with fire and swirling Glory. "Witches? Ha! You know nothing of us or who we are." The other men in the tavern turned their heads and rose from their seats at the sudden commotion. Proudly, Kole directed everyone's attention to Nettle, though the barkeep felt it wise to not stare at her as closely as he had before. "This is a bluebell faerie before you! Speak to her—and I in her presence—as you would to the Gods." Kole spat upon the countertop in drunken defiance.

The man spat right back; his own slobber hitting the same spot on the countertop. "Isn't it clear, bluebells, that the Gods no longer exist?"

Kole reached to the floor and scooped up a couple of the sparkling coins, still glowing from the faerie's enchantment. "Only witches it seems."

"Pfft. Be careful in what magicks you trifle with." The tavern was nearly silent aside from a scratching noise from the other side of the frosted window. It could have been an animal out in the cold or the creaking of the wooden framework. With eyes scrupulously scanning the empty spaces of the tavern, the barkeep lowered his voice. "The witch, she takes blood and flesh. Skin and hair and fingernails to keep her enemies forever near."

Kole wanted to dismiss his words, but there was definitely an underlying fear folded not so neatly within them.

There was a boarded-up door in the corner of the tavern, and he directed the girls' attention towards it. "She came through that very door one night. Apparently it is nothing but a staircase with a small stockroom at the bottom, full of grains and pickled preserves. I've never been down there. Where in that cellar she came from nobody knew, exactly. They said she burst from the door and ran right out there into the streets, eyes bleeding rivers. Room's been boarded up for more than twenty years now, and nothing more's come out of there since."

The scratching at the window intensified. There was a distinct tapping sound too, like a sharp talon upon thin glass.

Kole had always been fascinated by stories of witches, though she was not really certain if she ever believed in them. Her family forbade her from talking and asking questions about witches. But she did have a book hidden in her room, a book of ghost stories and dark fairy tales. She thought of that book and considered the details of it from her memory. The barkeep could read the curiosity easily on her face. "Girl, there are certain subjects one should not be fascinated by."

The two men who had stood from their seats had been

mumbling to one another in the background, but their discussion was quickly turning into an argument. A punch was thrown. Then another. Until the men erupted and rained blows upon one another. Blood flew from their knuckles. A darkness filled their eyes. And Nettle knew the ocean's anger was intensifying, pummeling the shores on the hunt for ever more wanton destruction.

She shook her own head and produced the pulsing light from her hands. The men wobbled a little before crumpling to the floor, stunned and blinded by the faerie's magick. She slammed back the glass of Glory in a prolonged display of power. The barkeep watched in stupefied awe.

There was a strength to the brew, and the faerie was not prepared for it. She had to hold onto the countertop to prevent herself from toppling over.

Kole helped her with an arm, and they hastily exited the unnamed tavern, leaving the money behind for the barkeep to do with what he wished. They stumbled drunkenly back out into the streets of Yarari, holding hands, swapping kisses, and cackling riotously. Their howling echoes might have sounded just like witches to anyone who did not know any better.

CHAPTER 13

Even asleep, Nettle could feel the sea smoke rolling in from the ocean. At first, its outer reach had merely licked and grasped at the shoreline, perhaps it was trying to pull the world itself into the water. Maybe it was trying to claw its way out. Eventually, the smoke rolled along the beach sand, creeping through the air like the tide, into the abandoned fishing village where it searched for something it could cling to. Any sort of life that might still be holding onto hope. There was no life to be found, not even birds above or grubs below.

And she felt it weave through each empty crack of every unoccupied home in the village before reaching farther; it crept over rocky outcroppings, hillside thickets, and brown, grassy knolls. Nettle winced as berry bushes wilted and deadened upon the smoke's arrival; she squirmed as the peeling birch trees in the marshland tried to bend themselves out of its way. Through dark woods, the sea smoke continued its path, eventually reaching colossal black cliffs, and from there it rose along rocky bluffs towards the town of Yarari. Most of Yarari's people appeared to be asleep, though the smoke passed by a couple of local men, still awake, and talking quietly of malevolent faerie girls who assaulted and impugned them before running wild and laughing madly through the streets. The men shifted uncomfortably as the smoke trickled past them.

A pair of ravens cawed aggressively from above.

From Yarari, the sea smoke—and Nettle's consciousness along with it—trickled into more woods, then down another hill until it reached a small clearing. In the clearing was a standing stone. The serpent shrine, some had come to call it. Hope lingered here; Nettle felt herself smiling a little at its power.

And there was more.

Surrounding the massive stone shrine was a field of newly-grown bluebell flowers, more than the eye could count. Their brilliant, violet chroma seemed to want to repel the smoke, as if darkness and dread were naturally opposed by such delicate flowers.

And the faerie sensed even more, still.

High up in a tall tree, beyond the sea smoke's reach—and seemingly even its notice—a thick branch grew. The branch pointed toward the sea. And clinging to the underside of the branch was a wooden orb. It glowed a little; a faint, otherworldly amber-pink glow.

Nettle suddenly realized her eyes were open and she was standing below the tree branch, beneath the tucked-away wooden sphere. A life vein cocoon. Tiny clucks at her feet, she looked down to see Talem once more. And though he had no head to speak of, she knew he was looking right at her.

Nettle took the chicken in her arms and followed the sea smoke into the dark woods.

It was a long walk. Nettle kept herself preoccupied by telling her story to Talem. She held the bird in her arms as she spoke of the satyr's orchid garden and his stubby horns. She remembered how much she loved winter's frozen streams and how they looked just like sheets of stone under the starry night skies of Sceanth. She fondly recollected a story of her mother, Cleo, and how they once spent an entire morning arranging river stones by colors and patterns, and then they eventually flew high above the river to admire their work shining beneath the sun rays and water ripples. Her mother taught her how to craft a life vein cocoon, and Nettle always felt she might have done it wrong because her mother never told her anything about the unsettling dreams she could expect. Nettle regaled the bird with a tale of her secret adventures into the Forest of Redd, where she and the voros moths would play tricks on the glimmer giants, using their magicks to make the foolish yet fearsome creatures think they misplaced their feasting prongs and other personal artifacts. Over and over she did this, not fearful at all of ever being caught, nor wary of what might have happened if she were.

It was invigorating to set certain thoughts free from her mind, to share her feelings with Talem while knowing the bird had no cognizance of any of it. *Buk-bawk*, was all that came from Talem, from wherever it was a headless chicken might cluck.

But Nettle did not tell tales of Piper, because she did not presume the chicken might understand the complexities of love. Of how much it can hurt.

Nettle was partly through another story when she stopped herself. She was recollecting a memory of flying through thick mist. It was so cold. Freezing. Eventually, through the darkness she saw an ocean materialize, and a capsized boat on the choppy water. There was a man clutching on to the boat, calling out for help. This was when Nettle stopped speaking. As though she'd lost her voice. This was not her memory, but the story Kole had told her about her grandfather being rescued at sea. He was rescued by an angel, she said. Nettle knew for sure if she allowed her mind to play out the rest of the tale, she would only see herself lighting her way through the dark, saving the man, and bringing him to the shore where she would restore his strength and return his life with a kiss. She didn't tell the rest of the story, however. Partly because she was confused about owning the memory of it, but also because of the voice she heard.

"They. Watch," a scratchy voice spoke slowly, with words far apart.

Nettle turned her head and perked her ears. There was only a row of gnarled trees before her; behind them was a great moon, finally free from the sea smoke's incessant obfuscation. But there was no indication of where the voice had emanated from. Unsatisfied, she looked at the bird in her arms.

The words slowed even more. "They. Watch. You."

"Talem—?"

"*Buk.*"

Nettle's shoulders dropped. Ahead, blacker than the night's black sky and as dark as dead space, was the familiar shape of the Obsidian Revenant. Though not on an island's precipice— and now the biggest thing in these woods—the tree continued to reach straight up for the stars, like summoning dark things, perhaps a conduit to the evil reigning down upon the world. Its thick, exposed roots seemed to writhe like a serpent when she was not looking directly at them. Only in her peripheral. But Nettle was not comfortable with keeping the Obsidian Revenant in her peripheral; its stark black surface made it hard to look away from it. The gap in its shadows materialized again, immediately bringing to mind her slipping inside the monstrous thing and waking up on the beach outside the fishing village. But she would not attempt to enter the tree this time, as long as she could remain in control of her own decisions, that is. She lowered Talem to the dirt and stepped cautiously towards the tree. Kole was wrong when she spoke about not being able to see the Obsidian Revenant. She said, "*You feel it. You dream of it.*" And yet, there it was. Again.

Unless Nettle truly *wasn't* seeing.

Hovering a hand closer to it, she once more felt the susceptibility of the tree's immense power. She did not know what it wanted, but she did know it was trying to draw her closer. The fuzzy shape of her hand reflected back at Nettle, though it was a much darker version of her own. At first it was formless until its shadowy film became clearer—almost too clear, for the hand had aged and grayed. Long, curled nails, scrapes and scars, and jagged wrinkles inside the palm appeared.

Was she seeing or dreaming?

If this were a dream, when would it end? And where did it ever begin? Perhaps it was everything from the very moment Nettle woke on Erw, back when she woke in the bed of the empty house in the woods.

The reflection acted independently; first the fingers splayed before bending talon-like. And then, impossibly, it burst out through the surface of the Obsidian Revenant. The hand seized Nettle's wrist, gripping it tightly. And again, a voice said: "They. Watch. You."

Nettle turned back to Talem and the chicken instantly turned to dust, blowing off in a streak of gray into the dark woods. Nothing marked its existence but a pair of fork-like prints in the dirt.

The grip on her arm tightened, though Nettle did not struggle, for she knew she did not have the strength to break free. She knew. "Who are you?" she asked the tree.

"Who—?" A figure appeared within the black bark, swirling within the darkness at first before coalescing into an old woman. Hair like seething, petulant ocean tides. A cavernous mouth of missing teeth. "I…am…not—" she spoke, as if drawing some strength from the words themselves. "—not what you think." Her words were heavy and piercing enough to cut rock. Her face formed dark mountainous veins and even darker valleys of creases and wrinkles. She had no eyes, merely twin pits of abyss in their place. This woman shook her head slowly at the faerie in her grasp, and her features became more ghostly as her face moved from side to side, as though she was fading in and out of reality. "Who am I? I am death in life and life in death. I am part of the cycle, and the circle's unseen corners. I am the lost memories of oceans. It is *Who are you?* that is the real question."

"I am Nettle. And I am not of this world."

"Yes…" The woman wheezed out her reply as though recollecting the name from a long-lost ledger. She released her grip from the faerie and brought her hand back into the tree. Again, her movements made her image become more ethereal. "I watch you," she said, and there were piercing caws from above. When Nettle looked up, she saw two ravens—one of black and one of white—perched on either side of the Obsidian Revenant like feathered gargoyles. "*They* watch you."

"These are Eamonn's birds."

"They watch *him*, too."

Nettle's arm felt numb, there was a frozen chill upon her where the woman's hand had been; some of her flesh had burned right off. It wasn't hurting though, just cold. She was feeling colder, ever colder.

Nettle recalled Eamonn's mention of the Erw Witch. And also the words of the barkeep back in Yarari: "*Be careful in what magicks you trifle with,*" he said. "*The witch, she takes blood and flesh. Skin and hair and fingernails to keep her enemies forever near.*"

"You are the creature that burst from the cellar, aren't you?"

"Perhaps. Some have called me a witch."

"Is that what you are?"

"Whatever you wish me to be, that is what I am." Her image swirled inside the tree, almost like she was willing to change into whatever it was Nettle wanted. The faerie only needed to ask. Even the woman's voice changed, becoming more scratchy. "Creature. Witch. Demon. Faerie. What is it that you wish me to be?"

"I will stick with witch. I have not met a witch before."

"Not ever?" The woman's face grew closer, her features more defined. Her black hole eyes pierced Nettle's very soul. "Why so certain are you? I would not be."

Nettle broke her gaze from the image in the Obsidian Revenant and turned out to the realm of Erw surrounding her. "Certainty is not a quality the bluebell faeries have passed on to me. Mostly, I find myself uncertain of this world. Might you tell me the reasons why Erw acts the way it does? Its ocean and its sinister smoke. The great serpent. This tree."

"All of it—?" The ravens leaned in closer to Nettle, as if questioning her themselves. "Who am I to answer for all of it?"

"I am certain *you* are the key."

"Tell me, do you talk to this land?"

"I try. It speaks differently out here. Different…from where I come from."

"Sceanth."

"You know of Sceanth?"

"I am…familiar. With many lands. And many creatures. Of the bluebell fae and the tricks they play."

Again, Nettle found herself recalling her adventures into the Forest of Redd with the voros moths, to use her magick to fool the glimmer giants. "Tricks—?"

"Some you are not yet aware of." The ravens laughed a cackling caw. "But you asked of this land and of its ocean. And where would my manners be if I did not answer?"

"Are manners a virtue of witches?"

She stopped; she hung on to the question, considering an answer. "If that is what you wish." Nettle felt the witch was speaking in riddles. It reminded her too much of conversations with Brawn; how he seemed to hint at the things he suspected she wanted to hear, rather than simply sharing his truths. "But let me tell you of our ocean. Our ocean destroys. All it knows is destruction. All it wants is suffering. And all that can stop it is the serpent. The serpent always returns." She said the words with some degree of vitriol. "It always does."

"I have seen the great serpent. In my dreams."

"Tell me, what is a dream but merely the truth trapped behind closed eyes? Some dreams are real while some are reality. And the difference? The difference does not matter at all."

"I tire of your riddles."

"So leave then," the witch hissed. Nettle stepped back. But not because she wished to; it was more like her control of her body was not her own. "Go on and leave this realm of Erw now, faerie. But know that if you do, you also break the circle. We are all a part of this. The serpent and the ocean. The girl down at the shrine."

"Kole—?"

"She is part of the circle. Without her, the circle would be broken. Incomplete. Your presence here matters, as does hers."

Nettle paused to consider this creature, her words and her riddles. "But what is *your* aim here, Witch of Erw?"

"I aim to break it all. To break the cycle once and for all. And the blindfolded fool has already unwittingly helped me."

"Eamonn—? What has he done?"

"Tried to kill the Revenant, he has. To save a love, he thinks." She reached a hand up and, from somewhere, pulled a shadowy veil over her face. "Presumes I cannot see his actions." The two ravens cawed once again, one playing off the other. Impossibly, their colors seemed to become clearer in the darkness of the tree. They took on new shades, both of them closer to blue: one of space, the other of frost. "But the man is lost in his *own* dreams. Just like you. There is danger to be found in other worlds." Just as Nettle's mother had said. "And worlds will poison. And dreams will only worsen."

Nettle took another step back. "I don't know what to do," she whimpered to herself. She missed her mother more than she thought she might. It was not supposed to feel this way upon emerging from her cocoon.

With a wave of both hands, the witch sent the ravens away. The birds flew from the Obsidian Revenant, disappearing once more. "Do what you must. Choose carefully, though it matters not in the end."

And then the Erw Witch screamed an awful, cackling scream. She screamed with a mouthful of hot, black blood.

Nettle felt the beads splatter her face before the world went dark. She felt she was falling, though in truth, she was having a difficult time feeling anything at all. In her head, her mother asked: *"Have you chosen your life veins carefully, Nettle?"*

CHAPTER
14

Nettle woke with a start. She was shaken by her dreams, and it took longer than it should have for her to realize where she was; no longer inside nightmares.

There was a hot breath on her cheek. Nettle's head was foggy from the effects of the Glory, her thoughts and memories and visions all shifting, slippery sorts of things, but she was inside a life vein cocoon. Kole was there, too. The girl's face nuzzled into Nettle's own, and the two of them were curled up together. The stale air within the cocoon smelled of too much drink. Its concave walls hummed with the echoes of their affection.

They hung upside down, the faerie and the fisher girl. Kole's calloused fingers entwined with Nettle's dark lilac hair. The green serpent tattoo almost curled around a sharp finger and faded kisses. Wings—even more iridescent inside the cocoon— cradled Kole softly, yet still held her firmly enough that there was the swell of bone beneath taut skin. Nettle hummed an otherworldly tune, something from her youth she'd forever sung on instinct; its words indiscernible yet haunting. There was a truth in the song, as though remnants of Glory still lingered on her lips and tongue.

Nettle was uncertain what had transpired between herself and the Erw Witch—whether the encounter with the soul inside the Obsidian Revenant really occurred or not—but she did not wish for this quiet moment to end, so she tightened her protective hold on Kole. She told herself she would stay like this until the girl woke and kept her eyes open lest she slip into dark dreams once more.

"They're wonderful," Kole gasped upon seeing the field of bluebells in the clearing. The flowers surrounded the serpent shrine, each one casting a tiny, quivering, wind-blown shadow upon the next. "And you say these are identical to those which grow in your own world?"

Nettle looked around the clearing tentatively; like a certain terror was waiting for her to let her guard down. Talem had returned—they'd seen him the moment they planted their feet upon the ground—and he was at the edge of the clearing, still headless, and standing on one foot then the other and back again. "The same. But their reasons for growing here now…it confounds me. And their number, there must be—"

"Three thousand, at least."

Nettle's eyes glanced around her feet, dumbfounded. "How do you come to know that?"

"I counted how many in an area, and then multiplied by how big the clearing is. It's just mathematics, Nettle."

"I do not understand these mathematics. What magick are they?"

Kole smiled. "We are taught to use stuff like that in fishing, when casting nets in different parts of the ocean. You're not in your homeworld anymore, Nettle. Not everything here is magick. But it *is* beginning to feel that way."

Above them, the cocoon hung; split in two and dangling

open like an empty walnut shell. "Kole, I am sorry, but I do not remember much about what occurred last night." She did not wish to mention her encounter with the Erw Witch. Not yet.

Kole crouched down to inspect a couple of the violet bulbs. Nettle fluttered closer and knelt down beside her, a warm, glowing hand on the girl's dithering shoulder. "I don't know what happened, either." Kole's voice was small and scratchy. "You said you gave me a gift, back before we left for Yarari. My hands feel tingly. Scratchy. Have you given these gifts to other humans before?"

"You are the first. Gifting a human is a special occurrence, and it does not happen for every bluebell faerie."

"And...what *is* my gift?"

"It's many things, really. We share a bond now, for one. I have given you my dreams, too. And also *that*." Without taking her eyes off Kole, the faerie gestured towards the life vein cocoon above them, thinly concealed by the still-lingering sea smoke. "And more, too. Likely more."

"Likely? You mean you don't know?"

"Not exactly, no. It can be hard to tell what they will all lead to, these gifts. But my dreams have told me some of it and they will tell *you* some of it, too."

Kole's body felt warm. "I feel sort of numb, as though a part of me is missing. Like a chicken without a head." Talem *buk-bawked* in the distance. "Is there anything you *can* tell me?"

The faerie bit her lip, with dagger-sharp canines Kole had not spotted before. "That is not for me to say. It is up to the dreams. I'm sorry, Kole. I cannot say more." Nettle tried to spy the cocoon up in the tree, but even the tree was now washed away by the smoke. There was a chunk of the cocoon—like a dish-sized piece of an egg shell—at her feet. "Tell me, do you recall what it was you dreamt of up there? Were your dreams beautiful? Wondrous? Frightening?"

Kole paused. "I...I don't think I dreamt of anything." She stared at the beautiful faerie in front of her. Nettle sensed her digging into and prodding at her own subconscious, as though splaying a deck of cards, and trying to identify the one card that was missing.

"Think about it, Kole," Nettle urged. "I have given you my gift; given my *dreams* to you. Obscured they may be—like this world in its mist—but they are there if you know how to look. Close your eyes."

Kole did. The Glory still raced in her head; its glowy light confusing her consciousness.

Nettle bent down and took the piece of broken cocoon into her hands. She brought it to her own face and took in the smell of it. "Feel with all of your senses: can you smell the fading essence of juniper and elderberry upon the air? Can you taste the cinnamon and frost lingering within unseen pockets of space?"

She wanted to tell Nettle she didn't sense any of those things, but she was too afraid to admit it. Still, Kole kept her eyes shut and tried her best to keep digging. All she could sense was the thunder of the far-off ocean. And shadows.

Nettle took a hold of Kole's hand and placed it upon the cocoon shell. "Is there an image of someplace else forming in your mind?"

The shadows in Kole's mind thickened. Into a gray-black muck of nothingness.

"Do you sense *anything* at all?"

And then she did. "Darkness?" Kole spoke, maybe questioning what it was she was now experiencing. She explained, as best she could, how she could hear the drip, drip, dripping of some distant water, from the inauspicious tips of cavernous stalactites. She *heard* it. She could smell the minerals pooling in the rock surrounding her. She *smelled* it. "I'm in total darkness." She kept her eyes closed. "I take a few steps, and slowly make out the shine of moisture on rock, like I'm in a deep cave. Am I casting this dim light myself? There seems to be a path. A tunnel. I think I'm going upwards?" Slowly, uncontrollably, Kole scraped her fingernails across the smooth surface of the broken cocoon shell. "And farther, just a bit farther ahead, there is a hole in the wall. I look into the hole and see mist; nothing but the sea smoke. As thick as it ever is. It taunts and torments, but I squeeze myself through the opening nonetheless." She gripped the shell tightly, as if her very being depended on it.

"Have you stepped through," Nettle asked.

"Yes."

"Turn," Nettle urged her. "Turn around in your mind. What is it that you see?"

A cold wind cut through her. The ocean roared and seaspray burst from somewhere around her. She was standing on a high peak. Kole did not know anymore if she were piecing a dream together or if she were experiencing something more. She could not release her grip on the cocoon; she tried to pull away but could not sever the connection. She found the strength to turn around. She looked behind her, toward the hole she just pushed her body through, and saw a tree. As black as thunderclouds and tar, and as murky as fear and space and death.

"The Obsidian Revenant—?" Kole knew she didn't have to ask.

"Yes."

Eyes still closed tight, Kole asked, "This is the same tree you saw, wasn't it? On the hidden island?"

Nettle did not say a word, yet somehow answered still.

"How can this be a dream then? Whether yours or mine…it doesn't make sense." Kole blinked her eyes open, lids fluttering as though waking from a hard slumber. "You *did* visit the tree, did you not?"

"Conscious or otherwise, maybe our dreams can take place in both states? Our speculations and trials might exist in either plane. Who can say if we are not still dreaming now?"

Nettle glided closer to Talem. The bird had remained in place, swaying a little back and forth, offering no answers of his own. She knelt in the bluebells, and placed her palm on his back. Already, her encounter with the Erw Witch was beginning to feel less and less like it had occurred. "I think we need to return to Eamonn."

"Without evidence of the tree?" Kole asked, nodding her

head towards the chicken. "Was that not its task? To find the Revenant?"

"I am not certain if Talem's purpose was to lead us to the tree." She looked up at Kole, still not yet prepared to speak of her earlier dream. And still not yet certain why. "Or if there is much more he was meant to show us."

"Like what?"

Nettle huffed a little to herself. "I do not mean to speak in riddles, but I believe we need to keep looking." She pulled a bluebell from the ground, took in its fragrance as though it were a long-lost friend, and gracefully tied the stem around Talem as a necklace. "It's the way things seem to work when you find yourself in other worlds."

"How's that?" Kole asked.

"The unexpected paths are sometimes the ones that take you to places you've already been."

Before leaving, Kole took a moment for herself at the serpent shrine. It seemed she still had some scraped-together hope left for the great serpent. She knelt before the stone altar, closed her eyes tightly, and mouthed some words for something. For hope? Providence? Or maybe just to remember what her place in her world once was.

Still sitting with Talem among the bluebells, Nettle watched her. Nettle did not know the reasons for praying, for keeping faith, or for having an enormous sea-bound deity to place hope within. The people of Erw were certainly different from the many enchanted creatures of Sceanth. Even the humans on Sceanth, they were so much simpler than these here. Her thoughts of Piper were fleeting, and the memory of leaving Brawn for the last time barely stung at all anymore. Visions of her own mother fluttered through her mind, passing like prickly brown samaras spinning to the forest floor from trees. Nettle did manage to recall how her mother would sit upon the tallest of outcroppings along the riverbank and stare endlessly with her mossy-green eyes, following one ripple after another as they snaked in and out and along the river's current.

Impossibly, a crack formed in the sea smoke above them, a needle of sunlight hit a bluebell just in front of Nettle. The flower glowed in the light and reflected its sparkle off the surrounding mist. It was only momentary, as Erw's sinister sea smoke was quick to reseal itself. But the moment was enough.

Nettle tightened the knot on Talem's bluebell necklace. She stroked the chicken's worn, dirty feathers before rising, and she joined Kole at the shrine, once again taking the girl's hand into her own.

When they did leave the shrine hand in hand, they left failing to have noticed the pattern formed by the bluebells. Truthfully, it was a pattern that might only have been noticed from high above: the flowers had grown in the same shape as the tattoo on Kole's neck. A winding serpent of lilac bloom twisted around the similarly-shaped stone altar. And if the girls had looked even closer, they'd perhaps have noticed that each and every one of the bluebells had grown out of the ground from a tiny bird's skull buried in the dirt. Ravens, chickens, and all manner of avian variety. And each tiny skull contained the dwindling echoes of terrible, haunting laughter.

CHAPTER

15

ONCE MORE, NETTLE FOLLOWED KOLE ALONG A TWISTED, unseen path towards Eamonn's home. The faerie continued to hold Talem in the safety of her arm. Erw's sea smoke was not following them, though the ravens had kept close, and no longer masked their presence, as if purposefully taunting the girls. Daring them to keep moving through the woods. Crossing mossy logs, the girls found the stone staircase in the familiar grove where the crooked, gnarled tree with the bones in it writhed out of the ground. The piece of driftwood that had previously covered the entrance was nowhere to be seen.

They descended the steps into the darkness. While Nettle knew her glow was dimming slightly, she could also feel Kole's own aura growing. Not enough to shed any light in the underground tunnel, but it was brimming beneath her surface. She smiled to herself, unsure if a smile was warranted. They came to the wooden door. The air still smelled strongly of the ocean—though there was another smell there, too. It smelled of grass and dirt. But also, the lurking stink of something dreadful. She picked at some dried, curling algae on the wood with a finger, but her finger was no longer as sharp as it had once been. Her skin was softer too, and the roughness of the door hurt as her palm caught on a splinter.

Nettle went to open the door, but Kole threw an arm across to stop her. She pointed above them and said, "Look."

The ceiling in the tunnel was not very high so it was easy enough to spot the fist-sized cloth bags hanging overhead; four of them in total, forming a near-square shape. Both girls were certain the bags were not there before. The pouches were pinned to the dirt above with sharp wooden stakes. These were certainly where the other smells had been emanating from. Kole reached for one and pulled it down. The bag was wet in her palm. "Are these meant as warning signs or are they some sort of arcane medium?"

"I couldn't know," was all Nettle said. Her first thought, naturally, was of the Erw Witch in the black tree.

Kole pulled the string loose and opened the bag. It did not contain bits of earth, as they might have suspected, but rather a mass of something organic and unrecognizable instead: black, sticky, and reeking. Like a tiny heart or a squishy sea creature. Callously, Kole tossed it against the wall and it stuck there for a brief moment before plopping onto the ground, sinking a little into the dirt.

Nettle tried the door and, its sheer weight aside, she pulled it open without difficulty. Her dulled glow was enough to shine upon a couple of candles, and Kole lit them with a nearby matchstick. The small room beyond the threshold was deathly in its emptiness; in much the same state as the girls had last seen it, prompting them to imagine the possibility of Eamonn simply vanishing altogether. It was not outside the realm of possibility. Nettle placed Talem on the floor, and he returned to peck at the familiar pile of the bones in the corner.

Nettle crouched at the end of the bed, inspecting one of the large stones keeping the covers secured to the dusty floor. Suspiciously, it was even heavier than it had appeared. She smelled it closely, and it carried the scent of something sad, like it contained a certain amount of grief and loss within it. In the next stone she sensed anguish, and in the next, despair. Beside the bed, in the corner, she reached for a few more bones which were piled up. She put her tongue to them, but was immediately baffled by their origins, and perhaps, their purpose too. Kole kept an eye on the faerie's behavior, no longer out of mistrust or uncertainty, but more in wonder of her extraordinary abilities. Nettle imagined Kole soon finding herself sniffing rocks, licking and tasting both the living and deceased creatures of Erw.

On the table, Kole rummaged through bird seed and broken, rusted curios. And she heedlessly flipped through thin, peeling books which appeared to be nothing more than some instruction manuals and various story collections. She blew some air out in frustration.

"Is something the matter?" Nettle asked, placing the bones back in the pile just as she found them.

"Eamonn wrote books of prophecies. Hand-written journals of sorts."

"He spoke of them," Nettle confirmed.

"Aye. And there was that sliver of the Obsidian Revenant he'd held on to." Futilely, she dug around the table more. "I can't find any of it here."

"Did he take these items with him?"

Kole shrugged. *Why would he?*

Nettle stood up and folded her arms together. "The Obsidian shard—it gave me a strong sense of unease when last we were here. When Eamonn held it out for me to take, I could not find the strength to do so. It...*pained* me. Not only did it hurt to set my eyes upon it, but to be in its very presence."

"And—? What are you saying, Nettle?"

"Now I do not sense it at all. But perhaps *you* can."

Kole closed her eyes. She tried to perceive what it was Nettle had described. A lingering unease. Pain. "I'm not feeling anything. I'm not—"

Thoughts raced through Nettle's head; ones she did not wish

to think. Memories of the hollow promises she'd made to Piper, and of seeing her father for the last time. Of Erw's furious ocean and its creeping smoke that had wormed its way into her psyche. She replayed her terrible dreams and the many deaths— the *countless* deaths—she'd experienced within them. All in the hopes of helping Kole sense what the faerie could not.

"Wait," Kole spoke suddenly, in a hushed tone. "Over there. That wall." She pointed at one of the tapestries on the wall. It was the same one Eamonn had stared into. Blue patterns and circles, difficult to make out before, but now Nettle could clearly see a bluebell in the center of it. A lonely, fading bluebell. She pulled the side of the tapestry away from the wall and there was an alcove small enough for only a thin shelf. On the shelf were the journals Kole remembered, as well as the ominous piece cut from the Obsidian Revenant.

"Not one of his better tricks," Kole commented on the hiding spot. The black shard hummed an unsettling sort of white noise. It shined a shadowy glow. Darkness and light in one. Both girls agreed that touching the sliver of the tree was out of the question. There were three dusty journals stacked upon the shelf, and Kole reached for the top one.

Flipping through the journal, she read aloud some of Eamonn's scrawled thoughts. They had all been ordered numerically.

Entry 306

"Though Harker had come from the posh manors of Upper Porteous, she had a natural way with others in my village. She made them feel safe. Myself especially. And she loved the woods more than anyone. And a good thing she did. Perhaps if it weren't for her carefree whistling through the muck and mire that day, I may have been lost in the Obsidian forever. I am quivering just thinking about it and writing about it now—that first time I'd discovered the Obsidian Revenant; how the tree wished for nothing more than to pull me into its darkness. How likely was it that the Erw Witch would have taken me then and there? She may have, too, if not for Harker's timely intervention, snapping me out of the hag's mesmerizing

glare. In an instant, the damned tree was gone. And in its place remained the sea smoke—but also that insouciant girl with the long braided hair, the elegant dress that was muddied up to her knees, and the bewitching sparkle in her eyes."

Entry 318

"She enjoys working with her hands. Her father might puncture me with a shell-splitter if he knew she was out in the fishing village constructing boats and cutting up her pristine, snowy knuckles. She is fearless. Accompanying me into the woods to fell trees for more building materials. Harker has become quite used to the tempestuous ocean and its destructive fury. The one force she seems more unsure about is the serpent. When it returned to chase the sentient waters back—as is its natural role in our realm—Harker simply could not bear witness; like its very presence was somehow wholly offensive to her. Have I been wrong for seeing the great serpent as a sign of hope? This time, she fled the village upon the serpent's arrival, and I followed her deep into the woods, all the way to the Black Cliffs. I followed her until she led me right to the Obsidian Revenant. I knew it to be the same tree I'd encountered before, yet this was not where I had been the first time. As though the thing could appear wherever it chose. From beneath its monstrous branches, and within its all-consuming shadow, Harker held me with calloused hands. And I professed my love for her."

Entry 342

"After a time, as the sea smoke once again cleared, so too did visions of my future with Harker. We found a tiny isle—halfway between Erw and Porteous—and upon it sat a lighthouse. From a distance, the lighthouse loomed out from the horizon, either like the healing horn of a unicorn or a horrible growth from the gnarled back of some great and frightening beast. Depending on one's disposition, I suppose. The lighthouse's purpose had been rendered obsolete due to the absence of boats making passage. And anyway, there had not been sea smoke in the realm for months now, not since Harker agreed to be mine. It was there on that rock, in front of that lighthouse and the crashing, angry waves, where we were wed. Strangely, she spoke of the Obsidian Revenant in her vows."

Entry 397

"There are worlds beyond this one. And in every world there exists an in-between place. Sometimes that place is an arcane patch on the forest floor; an unlived-in room in the back of a house; crossing through a doorway that never seems to close fully. And in every world there is a forest. And those who find themselves lost will find themselves there, impossible to ever know for certain if they have gone from simply knowing of and dreaming of another world to finding themselves lost within one."

Entry 411

"Last night, Harker told me she'd seen the Obsidian again. This time, she found it in the woods, in a grove I'd never known, but a grove I no doubt believed existed. She quivered in my arms as she re-lived it. I am trying as best I can to remember her story, but it is already fading tragically from me, just as the tree faded when Harker first found me. It called to her, she said. It seemed more monstrous than ever. She touched the horrible thing, and both the tree and my lady screamed into the night. They wailed for all the creatures who had lived and have died and will live again."

Entry 412

"Tonight, the ocean took Harker from me. But I know the ocean is not to be blamed. I will find that grove, and I will find that black tree, and I will take a piece of it, just as it took the only piece of me that ever mattered."

Entry 430

"I dreamt of her again last night. She walked through the woods, through the sickly trees themselves, as though she were a ghost. I fail to believe she is a ghost. In my dream, her finely braided hair was now unkempt. Her body mostly gaunt and sallow. Her eyes a burning golden glow, like the whole world was on fire within her. She wore the same elegant dress she wore when we first met, and I watched—crouched and hidden inside a shadowy bower—as she slithered through the woods' broken boughs. She stopped at something on the ground that I could not see, and as she bent to pick it up, she disappeared from my sight. Swallowed by the world around her. Around me."

"If my Harker can so easily find this Obsidian Revenant, then I need

only use the tree itself to find her. And I will see her again, outside of specters and ghostly dreams."

Kole put the book down and grabbed the next one. Flipping through the flimsy pages, she commented, "These are just his diaries; didn't Eamonn speak of writing premonitions? Prophecies?" The entries she skimmed through in the second journal were dated even further back. "They do not appear very helpful."

"But he knew of the witch," Nettle said. "And he was aware of the Obsidian. And of the tree's strange power. What about how his wife seemed to be drawn to it?"

The girl reminisced. Harker had been in the village since before Kole was born. "Harker was always a bit strange. She was nice enough to me, though. Just like he wrote in the journal, she *did* have a way of making us feel safe. Still…"

"Still—?"

But Kole didn't have any words to finish her thoughts. "How do you suppose Eamonn plans on saving her? She was taken by the ocean. Like everyone else."

"*Can* he save her?"

"He must have a way."

"Perhaps he does not, though."

"Nettle, you come from a land of faeries and giants! Your boyfriend was half-goat, and you still doubt the weirdness of *this* place? If there is a way for him to save Harker from whatever purgatory she's in, then Eamonn has already figured it out."

The two of them glanced at the Obsidian sliver on the shelf. Whatever light was in the small room felt like it was being pulled into the black shard. It still hummed eerily. A haunting tune in the girls' heads. There was an answer within it somewhere.

Talem questioned it. "*Buk buk-bawk?*"

Without pulling her eyes from it, Kole asked, "Do you wish to touch it, or should I?"

Nettle extended her arm and could plainly feel the sliver's darkness. She knew it wanted something from her. It wanted from Kole too, if only it could weaken one or both of them enough to draw them nearer.

"Maybe we should take it together? At once?" Nettle asked.

Without a word, Kole agreed. They reached for it cautiously, and in unison, each placed their fingertips upon it. Nettle still felt agony firing through her hand, her arm, and deep inside her body, though it was lessened by having Kole there. Their free hands found one another.

Kole fought to speak. "What…what is this—? It is inside my head."

"Follow the pain," Nettle urged. "See where it guides you."

"It feels like—like I am holding a part of me. A piece of myself."

"Listen to it, Kole. It speaks to you, yes?"

"It does." Straining, Kole listened to what was inside her head. "A woman's voice—" To Nettle, it was merely a warbled static. In an instant, the candles went out—both of them—conceivably absorbed by the Obsidian shard. Only a dull amber-pink glow from the both of the girls remained now, though Kole did not seem to notice the change in her body. Or if she did, she was putting it out of her mind for now. "I heard a woman. She was telling me to…return? Return to the place we were born on Erw. We—?"

"The witch," Nettle said. "She speaks to me. Her words are meant for me." The faerie recalled when she first woke on Erw, in the house in the wooded marshland. In a bed with a terrible wind blowing against thin windows and the as-yet-unknown ocean roaring in the distance. It was the dream that she still had yet to wake from. "I need to return to the house."

The girls released their hands from the Obsidian shard, and as they did so, the candles slowly flared back to life. Kole asked, "What house?"

"Where I woke. Before finding you."

"It is where Eamonn has gone?"

"What has become of Eamonn I cannot be certain. But I believe *that* is where I will find what I seek, Kole." With wide eyes of hope, Nettle turned to Kole. The faerie's eyes were less iridescent now, and more the color of robin eggs. "Will you come with me?"

Kole managed a smile. "I don't believe our being apart is a choice any longer, Nettle."

And taking the girl's hand into her own, the faerie said, "I don't believe so either."

CHAPTER
16

Bluebell faeries are known for their innate ability to find the places they search for. Whether it is into the unknown, or places they've fluttered through before; some only in forgotten memories, and even some in life vein cocoon dreams. For Nettle, navigation was never a strong skill, so she would use her connection with the voros moths of Sceanth to lead her into the unknown. Voros moths glow a little themselves, particularly when lighting the way for traveling companions, as though they are excited and content to do so. The long, fine filaments on their thoraces will glow like ember hairs plucked from the brows of glimmer giants. And intuitively, they always know where it is they are meant to go.

On Erw, Nettle could not recall the path she took from the house in the woods; retracing it was proving to be quite difficult. She hoped, ineffectually, that the very act of holding Talem in her arms would be enough to guide them properly. All the while, Kole kept asking her questions in failing attempts to verify their destination.

"I remember a densely wooded marshland. Birch trees. I followed a trail…"

"There aren't many trails in these woods, Nettle. The people of Erw are not much for adventures; we only go where we know how to get to. Exploring and making walking trails through the land is somewhat foreign. You said you spoke to a *slug?* And some berries? Why not get *them* to lead the way again?"

"The living things in this realm are not capable of leading me. They merely guide my senses in order for me to make decisions." Talem *buk-bawked,* perhaps taking offense to her statement. Nettle placed him back down in the dirt.

It was obvious Kole still found herself frustrated by the ways of the faerie at times. "Can't you do it again? Can't you allow your senses to be guided?"

"Like the rest of me, that ability seems to be changing." Empathy is a powerful tool for bluebells faeries. Nettle used to feel all the life surrounding her. The birds' merriment and joy. The river's distant sorrow. The cheerlessness of the dirt. She kept warm just by sensing the love from the flowers and the giant killorn trees around her. It was possible for plants to know love; one only had to talk to them. "Change has never been a thing of bother or inconvenience. But that part of me…I miss hearing the world speak."

There was a sadness connecting the girls; a particular gloominess not rarely known in Erw. Kole watched the faerie's movements as they kept on along their aimless course. "You have not been using your wings, Nettle."

Nettle looked down at her muddy feet, as though connecting two disparate thoughts. "I do not mind my feet on the ground." That was all she said on the matter.

In her heart, Nettle knew they needed to find the house in the woods. *The place where we were born on Erw.* But in her head, she could think only of her maddening dreams. The dark visions which had pricked her mind, her very sanity. All over again, even while awake, she experienced terrible things like bones falling from the sky. A witch bursting through a cellar door, full of sinister screams and wicked howling. Being trapped underwater in the fishing trawler and saved by the great serpent.

And then waking in the bed in the house hidden somewhere in these woods. Waking—? From *what*, though? It seems so long ago, fluttering through the lands of Sceanth to return to the life vein cocoon, just as she always had. To hide herself in order to lose herself in her dreams.

Nettle stopped taking steps, and she looked around—wherever she was—trying not to feel so small. "Kole? Is this… am I still…in a dream?"

Kole blinked, perhaps not comprehending the question fully. A wind not there a moment before suddenly picked up, rattling the web of branches above; the birch trees creaked.

"Have I woken yet? From whatever this is?"

The faerie held her hands out, and Kole took them, interlocking their fingers together. "This is no dream, Nettle."

"So a nightmare, then?"

"I wouldn't call it that. But I think what you're feeling—what it is that frightens you—is nothing more than the cycle of Erw."

The cycle, Nettle thought. The witch's words in the woods: *The serpent. The ocean. The sea smoke. The girl.*

And then Kole's eyes widened as though realizing all of her senses were suddenly acting differently. "And within it all is also the cycle of *us*, bluebell faerie." She said *bluebell faerie* like she was not herself; her words not her own; her true place somewhere not seen. Distant.

"*Buk—?*"

"Are you all right, Kole?" Still with fingers laced together, she gave Kole's hands a shake, and the girl returned, snapping back to reality.

Her eyes were unsteady and not at all focused on Nettle, watching the space around them instead. Searching for something which was absent.

"Kole—? What is it?"

"You told me about the moths of your world."

"The voros moths? But there are no—"

"Not the voros moths. Listen."

There was a nearly imperceptible static in the air. It grew louder. A humming. A buzzing. Through the spaces between trees, Nettle could see something coming. Its shape was a changing thing: fluid like the ocean's waves. At first an undulating ball, before stretching and thinning out like a taut rope, and then back again.

It was a swarm of black flies. Maybe only a few dozen, but the intensity of their buzzing gave the impression of hundreds more. One by one, they broke out and flew towards the girls and the headless chicken, each one sticking to the misty-wet bark of the surrounding birch trees. Their cloudy gray wings still hummed a resonance of darkness similar to that of the ocean's. The light in their shimmering burgundy eyes reminded Nettle a little of the light her own used to bear; the same light that was now burgeoning in Kole's eyes.

Inquisitively, Kole drew closer to a couple of the black flies on a tree. "Did...did I just summon these insects?"

"Just as you harnessed your abilities to seek the Obsidian shard in Eamonn's home, you've used them to call upon your world's creatures."

"And what—? These flies will show us to your house in the woods we seek?"

Nettle nodded. "They are not voros moths, but they should do."

The flies unstuck themselves from the birch trees and made for the woods. But slowly, slow enough for the girls to follow. "Aye," Kole said in wonderment. "They should do."

They treaded lightly through the woods, deeper and deeper, and following the mass of black flies. The girls held hands, and while Kole was clearly fixated on the abilities and changes within her, abilities which were growing by the moment, Nettle could not take her eyes off the fisher girl, and the sheer joy bursting from her. Nettle sensed it was an emotion Kole had not experienced often in the desolate fishing village of Erw.

And they followed the swarm until Nettle knew for certain where she was.

A trail appeared. Berry bushes with their rotted treasures, nothing more than stains upon the forest floor. And footprints: a faerie's trepidatious and curious exploration through a dark new world. The black flies ceased their forward motion and hovered in place.

"This is it," she said.

Kole took a second look around. "But—?"

"I know it, Kole. I was *here*."

"But there is no house."

Once more, the memory of waking in the bed returned to Nettle. The wind pressed hard against the thin walls and windows. She remembered hovering down the shadowy staircase. There were heavy, sour-smelling curtains in the foyer; the two charcoal drawings hung next to one another, one of the island and the other of a boat; the front door, slightly ajar and beckoning Nettle outside.

But she also recalled the dream borne from the black tree on the island itself: where the picture in her hands burst into flames and the house burned to the ground, consuming her, too.

"It *was* here. Those are my foot tracks in the dirt. You see them, do you not?"

Kole looked around. Trying to find—hoping to find—any clue to prove Nettle's story as truth.

"You see *me*, do you not, Kole? It is nothing but magick at work here. The witch…she plays with our senses! She—" The faerie hung onto her last words.

"Nettle? I don't see…Are you all right?"

Nettle placed a finger between both their lips, and lowered her voice. "There is a presence in the woods, Kole."

Branches and leaves rustled nearby. Sticks or bones or other sickly, brittle scatterings snapped apart.

"Who—?"

From the row of shadowy birch trees, a tall figure stepped forward, lumbering awkwardly as if injured. "Someone who does not hide as well outside of his buried home," the man said. The frayed cloth was still wrapped tightly around his head, covering his eyes.

"Eamonn?" Kole said. "You have followed us here?"

"Your light is not hard to spot," he said, hobbling closer. "When did you begin glowing anyway, Kole?" Eamonn carefully waved a hand through the girl's amber-pink aura. He turned to Nettle and pulled the cloth away from one eye. His eye was a weathered brown color, like sun-bleached driftwood. "And your *own* glow, faerie—it is much dimmer than I recall. He dumped his body into the cradle of an old, rotted stump. Talem waddled closer to his keeper, though continued to walk around in a small circle. "Something attacked me," he said. Pulling his foot from the shadows, the girls were horrified to see it was not much more than withered flesh and bone. Like some force grabbed hold of his leg, burning what it could of him.

"The Erw Witch." Nettle grasped her own arm, where her flesh had burned, too. It was still cold to the touch.

"The witch, you say?"

"Yes," Nettle replied. "She has been busy it seems. And her power grows."

"You think I don't know this? The ocean is wreaking havoc on the land." Eamonn turned directly to Kole. "Our village has been destroyed!"

"The village? It was not—"

"I was just there, Kole! I saw the entire beach consumed. Our homes smashed to smithereens. There is nothing left."

Nettle interjected, pointing an accusatory finger his way. "And it is *your* fault isn't it, Eamonn?"

"Me—?"

"The witch herself said as much. She told me *you* helped bring this madness."

Eamonn looked down at Talem, then glanced around the woods, his one uncovered eye wary of any movement or noise in their vicinity. He was quick to pull the cloth back over his face. "So you spoke to the Witch of Erw then? Perhaps it is *you* who has doomed us all?" Thick beads of saliva formed on his lips. He spit a little on his own shirt as his intensity flared, and he winced at a surge of pain in his ravaged leg. "It matters not, though. I don't care if that damned hag knows my aim."

"What *is* your aim, Eamonn? What is your agenda?" Kole asked accusingly. "You plan on finding your wife, don't you? You told us to find the Obsidian, but you already have, haven't you?"

There was no doubt the blindfolded man was staring directly at Kole. Perhaps searching for a way to not answer her question. "What is *your* agenda, girl?"

"I am merely helping the faerie," she said defiantly.

Eamonn laughed a little to himself, though the girls heard him clearly. "And the faerie? Has she figured out what it is *she* wants?"

"To destroy the Erw Witch," Nettle said adamantly.

"Destroy her? But…*why*? What purpose would that serve?"

Kole and Nettle searched one another, hoping the other would have the answer. "To break the cycle—?" Nettle asked. But who were they to decide these things, anyway? The world— and every world—was bigger than them, wasn't it?

"Destroying the witch will not break the cycle. Don't you see? It is what has been done forever in Erw. The ocean takes from us, the serpent responds. Hope returns. The witch drives the serpent back, only to be destroyed herself. It's all inevitable. And then it begins again. Killing her is only doing the very thing that is *meant* to happen!" He sunk his withered foot into the mud as deep as he could, trying to ease the pain. With one tired hand, Eamonn pulled the cloth from his face entirely now; both eyes were hollowed and red from tears. "I only wish to save my wife. Harker is my everything. I vowed I would find her."

Kole spat dismissively into the dirt. "The ocean took Harker, just like it took our entire village. Eamonn, you *know* she's not coming back. You know it for certain."

"What I do know means nothing. Like the tree itself has proven: when we are only too certain of something, it is quick to disappear. To fade from our grasp."

Kole said nothing in response to his words, and again, simply spat into the dirt.

Undaunted, Nettle sat herself next to Eamonn, crouching closely. Talem jumped back into her arms. "This witch. She told me you sought to destroy the Obsidian Revenant. You want to kill it? Why, Eamonn? Why kill something that is so alive?"

He turned and sneered, eyeing her up and down. "All trees are alive, faerie. You more than most should know this."

"But it is not just a tree. It is even *more* alive, like *us*." Nettle recalled the sensation of being near the tree, whether atop the hidden island or lurking around the serpent shrine. The uneasy feelings of evil and spite and pain that scratched her insides and dimmed her glow. But somewhere within it was the intricate patchwork of an actual life—of *many* lives, maybe—and it was not something that could so easily be purged from existence. In a land so dark, it, too, was a beautiful mark upon the world.

Eamonn continued. "What I didn't tell you before—what I couldn't describe to you out of fear of the witch knowing— was that I found the Obsidian again. It was colossal, even larger and blacker than I'd recalled. I knew I would find it, too, and I carried with me every axe and splitter I could. I sought to bring it to the ground. I was driven to hear its thunderous crash delivered to the earth! It took every blade I had, but that shard I cut—the sliver—it was all I could take from the monstrous thing."

The faerie's eyes widened. "But why would you—? For what purpose?"

Eamonn took a deep breath in, then released it very slowly. A gust around them picked up and rattled the branches and blew leaves across the path. Black hand-shaped leaves, just like the ones the girls had seen in the dead woods, scattered before them. "A boat." He scratched at his beard, and there was dried blood caked on his fingers and the back of his hand. "I've made many boats before but never from trees like that. It pained me with each attempted cut, such raw fury within it. But I kept at it because it was the only way. Just as Harker could find the tree, I would use the Obsidian Revenant to find *her*. But the Erw Witch and her cursed tricks are too strong."

A wind in the far distance scoffed at them all; there was a muffled cackling within the mist.

"And then," he continued, gesturing towards Nettle, "when this faerie appeared…I thought *she* might be the answer."

Kole finally found the words to speak. "Eamonn, nothing is hidden from the witch. And if you think so, you are a fool."

Eamonn laughed a huff of a laugh to himself and shook his head.

"What's so funny?" Kole asked.

With wobbling legs, he stood slowly, pulling his one wounded foot out from the mud. He tossed the cloth he'd been clutching into some dirt beneath the trees. "Girl, love is a thing of many wonders. Yes, it can make us perform many foolish acts. And while it hurts us in ways we'd never imagine would hurt, it also fills us with the most unexpected hope. But mostly, *you* have no idea about any of it."

Nettle was still sitting on the stump with the chicken in her arms, but she looked up and studied Kole closely. Kole turned to her, too. In an instant, Nettle read the many thoughts running through the girl's head. Kole considered all of the tales Nettle had told her. Of her boyfriend Brawn and her girlfriend Piper, and if the terms boyfriend or girlfriend meant anything at all to the bluebell faeries of Sceanth. She thought of the kiss they shared and the gift that had been passed between them. She thought of her own grandfather's story about being saved at sea and how he wished for his granddaughter to one day see an angel, too.

Without turning from Nettle, Kole answered Eamonn. "What are you waiting for then? You can go on back to looking for your wife. And we'll all keep believing what we believe."

"And so we will," he said in retaliation. The ravens cawed from somewhere above them and Eamonn hobbled back into the trees. "But remember," he called out. "Destroying the witch is inconsequential. In the end, her power is meaningless." The intensity of the birds' shrieks grew. There was an arrogance in the breeze, and an anger all around. "She is *nothing*. And she is not worth your fear."

The familiar scream suddenly burst from the sea smoke.

Eamonn collapsed to his knees as though he had been shot with an arrow and he turned back to the girls: his face was all searing red blisters. He gritted his teeth, trying to hold back the pain, but in less than an instant, Eamonn burst into flames. The birch trees around him lit up, too; their bark peeling away and blackening at the edges. A smoking, sticky mound of some bubbling tar-like substance was all that was left of the man, sinking slowly and dissipating into the mud.

The horrible cackle echoed off into the distance, with feathered wings flapping, and perhaps even the howling of some vanquished sea creature and the dwindling remains of hope.

"Gods—" Kole muttered to herself as she watched the remains of Eamonn disappear entirely. She reached a hand out behind her, maybe hoping the faerie might take hold, but only grasped at the air instead. Kole turned to find Nettle, who was already taking steps into the dense sea smoke. Without her glow, the faerie was quickly disappearing, too. "Where are you going, Nettle?"

She answered almost trance-like. "Back to the hidden island, I think."

Kole tried reaching out in the same way she summoned the black flies, but she felt nothing. "But how? We don't even know where—"

Nettle scanned above them for the ravens, but they were already taken by the night. "The witch wishes for us to find her."

And with the faerie's words, the sea smoke cleared enough to form a path, pointing back towards the fishing village. Nettle held out a free hand and Kole took it. Their touch warmed them both, and they kissed once more before venturing into what just might be the final unknown.

THOUGH THEY WERE FOLLOWING THE PATH DRAWN OPEN by the sea smoke, it was a path Kole must have walked a thousand times. There were certain feelings in her movements, in every step she placed upon Erw's muddied surface and the way she took in its air. She had a familiar connection with her world, similar, Nettle surmised, to the one that she herself had with Sceanth. Through a messy patch of dead brambles and multiple trees felled from a windstorm, Kole stepped over and crouched under obstacles at an instinctual pace. She hopped from the shallowest spots of muddy puddles. It was the way her palms brushed mossy trees and how her feet skipped across slippery rocks that her link to Erw was strengthened. Even the mist and the wind itself wound around the girl in their own discernable ways.

Kole's connection to this place was just so…it was obvious to Nettle that Kole had sensed something was off. When they eventually returned to the fishing village, the sea smoke dispersed some, and the ocean seemed to awaken, like a dog when its master returns. But this dog was restless and had a fire in its belly.

The village appeared just as it had when they left, with unlit lanterns outside homes, windows still shuttered, and doors closed tight, looking more like its people were hiding inside, rather than having simply vanished. They approached the same home Nettle had first entered days before, when she was attacked by the then-nameless fisher girl who had only been hoping her family might return. And just like then, Kole was still fooling herself into believing her family might yet be there, just behind the door. It wasn't fair, how wanton desire can so easily overcome the strength of memory.

Nettle took note of the fear in Kole's eyes as she paused. "What is it?"

"There's a presence here."

"A presence?" Nettle had carried Talem in one arm for most of the walk, her other hand still held on tightly to Kole's.

"Either still lingering, or not long removed. Not unlike when you first wandered through here. But where you came in casting a warm glow, this is decidedly opposite. Like a frigid darkness." She shivered quickly as if something had shot straight through her. "Do you not feel it, Nettle?"

There was *something* there worth sensing, something made of evil and vicious intent. Nettle let go of Kole and touched a palm to the door, but it too was stripped of feeling. Just a cold, dead piece of wood; its hinges nearly cracked in two from the constant battering of bitter wind and salt spray. Kole placed her hand upon the heavy door also, and pushed it open, once more stepping inside her abandoned home.

The girls agreed to stop at the village before venturing out to find the hidden island, mostly just for some supplies, such as lanterns and sustenance: bread, fish jerky, and drink. They were unsure if Talem required anything at all.

Inside, chairs and tables were tipped over, some split in two. Candles were strewn across the floor. Pictures that had once been displayed upon the mantle above the iron hearth were knocked down, lying amidst tiny bits of broken glass. The room stank. It was an earthy scent, mixed with something uncharted and unnatural. Kole had no immediate words for the mess and destruction. She looked at Nettle in partial disbelief, partial sadness, before exiting through a doorless archway into the kitchen. Thunderclouds rolled in the far distance.

As Nettle lowered Talem to the floor and lifted a chair in one corner back onto its feet, something dripped onto her shoulder. It was a thick, heavy plop and even through her dress, it immediately felt warm on her skin. She looked up and noticed a tiny pouch hung from the dark corner of the ceiling, a wet patch on the bottom of the cloth. The same as she'd seen hanging outside Eamonn's door earlier. It was out of her reach, so she fluttered up to inspect it; her wings strained a little from the effort of flying, even from such a short distance. Her toes reached for the floorboards. The bag was tied with a string and the string was nailed into the ceiling. It had the same ominous, evil sort of stink to it. Nettle touched the pouch with her tongue, and it tasted familiar, not in the way dirt and rivers and earthly creatures might be familiar, but more like the faerie held a personal connection to its contents. And just as another muddy globule formed on the bottom of the bag, something pricked Nettle's tongue. She spat blood onto the back of her hand; it was a swirling bead of luminous life force, glowing a little dimmer than it used to.

"*Buk buk-awk*," Talem spoke indifferently from below.

She wiped the blood from her hand onto her dress, now dirtied and stale from this world and its salty sea smoke, and planted her feet back onto the creaky floor. Nettle scanned the room and noticed a cloth pouch hanging from all four corners; the same muddy wetness dripping from each one. Something dark sealed within each and every pouch.

The photograph of Kole and her parents was on the floor, beneath its splintered frame and broken glass. Nettle crouched over the photo and looked into the fisher girl's eyes and her cracked smile. The faerie tried smiling the same smile. Then she folded up the paper and surreptitiously slid it into her dress.

Nettle headed for the next room, motioning for Talem to follow her. "Come," she said. The bird stuck an already-dirty toe into one of the muddy puddles on the floor before tagging along behind the faerie. But Kole appeared in the doorway first. She braced herself uneasily on the door frame, obviously shaken, by a memory, a dream, or something more tangible. There were tears in the corners of her eyes and dirt on her lashes.

Something on the floor caught her eye, and Kole stepped into the room. She crouched down and picked up a pointed metallic object. It was the spiral tip of her family's serpent altar. The bottom appeared to be missing, and Kole eventually placed the tip of the altar back above the hearth. It clunked heavily upon the wooden mantle.

Thunder roared again, though it could very well have been the ocean, for when they exited the home—with Kole carrying a small bag of supplies and Nettle again holding the headless chicken—the water had not-so-subtly crept right up to the door. It was angry, and its fury made the tide move faster than what should have been natural.

Nettle considered: if the satyr had made good on his flimsy promise of giving her the buried ocean of Sceanth, would it, too, have been so bent on destruction? Perhaps his shallow, un-promised vows had actually been made as some kind of favor to Nettle? She shook the thoughts from her mind and caught up to Kole, making sure the pilfered photograph was secure within her dress.

The wooden path that led from the village to the water was no longer visible, submerged by the seething, foaming tide. Kole noted the tide was much higher than usual. She focused on their destination, obscured as it was behind thick sea smoke; she knew instinctively from so many walks out to the boats, in the hopes it was finally the time she would be asked to help gather a fishing trawl and come aboard.

Up aways along the shore, still mostly grayed by the fog, the graveyard of boats remained rotting and sinking slowly into the sand. The ocean clawed closer and closer. Kole hoped any of the trawlers might be less wrecked than she recalled, but she knew instantly upon seeing them again that not one of the vessels would be seaworthy. Most anyone could tell, experienced or otherwise. She and Nettle both slowed their stride some as they approached, already unsure of just what it was they might do next.

"Could you not fly us over there, Nettle? You found the island once, already."

"But that was on my own. And when my power, when my strength was…fuller."

Kole's hand caressed the collapsed underside of one of the boats; Nettle continued to hold Talem in one arm but followed Kole's path along the wood with her one free hand. It was barely there, but she felt a still-lingering pain from the boat. A splintering of wood, buckling from a heinous force of nature. "These boats. They cannot take us, can they?"

"These ones…they came crashing onto the shore one by one. Only weeks apart." Kole explained to her how the bodies that were recovered from these last three boats had all been buried at the far edge of the village. "I helped my father. We silently shoveled dirt and rocks for days."

"Does your village have more boats?"

"We had another."

"And it—?"

"—is still lost at sea. My father's boat. It is out there—" she waved an angry, petulant hand at the ocean. "Out there somewhere. But the serpent watches over him. And my mother, she was frantic. She left only days ago in search of him. She ran from our home in the middle of the night."

The faerie tried to listen, but sensed she knew the truth— the reality of it all—far better than Kole had herself. Nettle's hand came to rest upon Kole's. "They seem to be strong vessels. These boats of yours. I'm sure the last of which has kept your family as safe as it could." The ocean was at their feet before they even realized it. The sea smoke was so thick around the girls now, their view of one another was becoming hazy.

Kole released her hand from the hull, but kept it wrapped safely within Nettle's. "Eamonn built many of our village's boats himself. I can still recall long days of fetching wood and felled trees from the forests with him and Harker. She was kind enough to me. Though something seemed to perpetually distract her thoughts."

"The tree, likely."

Kole nodded in agreement, though it was nearly imperceptible.

Water splashed above the girls' knees. The smoke irritated their skin, almost scratching them, tugging at them, whispering a horrible noise into their ears. Something within Nettle wanted to taste it; she wanted it to fill her mouth with its swirling madness; she needed to feel its darkness within her. She tried shaking these thoughts from her head, but they would not go.

Distant bells and wind chimes began clanging harder. Through the mist and beyond, the din of the crashing ocean shifted, almost as though it were making way for something.

And it was.

"A boat approaches," Kole spoke quietly, eyes wide. A heavy wave nearly collided with both of the girls, still managing to knock them back a few steps.

"From another village?"

"No," Kole mumbled as a silhouette formed. "This one is ours."

And indeed, a boat did emerge from the gray nothingness. It came in with the tide, cresting large waves, its impact upon the water reverberating through the ocean, through the land, through the girls. Its pair of tall masts were both split and broken, its sails flapping uselessly. Kole could not take her eyes off of it. She did not blink, even as both the torrential ocean spray and the smell of death hit her face. She did not flinch, even as the howling screams entwined in the mist surely raged through her mind. And she did not crumble, not even when she knew for certain it was her father's boat crashing onto the beach.

There was a horrible rending sound as wood bent and cracked, lurching into the sand and rocks; bits of the hull burst apart before the entire hulking vessel skidded and sank to a stop. Ocean waves continued to pound the stern, unsympathetic towards the damage already inflicted.

When Kole finally did try to move closer to the boat, Nettle's hand held her back. "I sense the dead aboard this ship, Kole. Suffering."

Kole shrugged her body away, more forcefully than Nettle expected. "I am not a stranger to suffering." She edged closer. Nettle and Talem followed. From the sand, they could see silhouettes on the boat, but not of the living. These were bodies tied to the masts—three of them from the looks of it—in various stages of decomposition. Purposefully, the sea smoke cleared enough for the girls to make out the horrible details. Some flesh and hair remained but it was mostly exposed bones and cartilage. The fishing nets fixed tightly around the carcasses were the only things keeping them together. Skulls still somehow raised high, defiant to their miserable end. Terror still frozen on their faces.

Everything was eerily silent. Nettle turned to Kole, who was frozen, too. The girl tried to gather her own breath but could not seem to find the right muscles. The nerves around her eyelids flickered, pulsated. Tears trickled like rain from roof trusses. Finally—uncontrollably, while still sobbing—Kole released whatever was left inside of her into the tide; it was a nightmarish, rancid stream of sickly black that mixed into the contemptuous ocean.

Nettle had to hold the shaking girl tight to keep her from collapsing entirely. "I—I'm sorry, Kole. This is a terrible thing to witness." Still, the faerie was morbidly curious about the arrival of the boat. And where it might have come from. "But why… why are these men tied to the ship?"

Not caring at all about the mess she left, Kole sunk waist-deep into the tide. Eventually, she caught her breath. She wiped her mouth. "I've read stories," she recalled finally, brushing sweat from her brow. "Stories of ravenous mermaids. Their songs were known to lure sailors, and the men—and women—would never be seen again. So, sailors would secure themselves to their boats so they couldn't jump into the water. It was the only way to resist the mermaids' songs. But my family urged me to only believe in the good stories. Mermaid and witch legends only serve to harm, while the great serpent…"

"The serpent is your hope. I know." Nettle could not help but think of her own mermaid dream, while she could only stare at the dead who were tied to the twin masts. "It appears as though they believed in *something* terrible. Something evil."

Kole asked, "Can you take us up to the deck, Nettle?"

The faerie took both Kole and Talem into her arms, and fluttered up over the railing, onto the deck of the fishing trawler. Her arms strained with the extra weight; her wings hurt, and her glow faded a little as she exerted herself.

Broken crates and barrels were strewn about the deck, loose netting, torn sails, and some supplies—jugs, knives, and harpoons—scattered into corners. The reek of death was worse here. Sea lice had colonized on corpses' legs, still consuming them from the waist-down, eating them from the inside out. The sight of these men was sickening, but Kole counted and confirmed there were merely three of them. "They fished in fours. Always with four men." She reached for a broken harpoon and poked at one of the carcasses, the sea lice barely took notice as they continued to consume what was left. The bodies were drained of life, almost beyond recognition. For what it was worth, Kole prayed silently for the souls of the men. After a moment, she said, "None of these are…*were*, my father." The knots on ropes holding the bodies to the masts were tied expertly. "Someone else had to have tied these men securely."

"Your father then?"

"Aye. And he must be out there still."

"How can you be so certain?"

"I cannot. It is only a feeling." She touched the serpent on her neck. "It is merely hope."

Nettle's palm also found its way to the tattoo. Her own hope was being placed along uncertain pathways. For the moment, she only wished to keep it tied closely with Kole's own—and yet Nettle was still finding it difficult to narrow down where it all might be headed, exactly.

Kole gave her head a shake. "How are we going to find that hidden island of yours?" Her fingertips gently slid across Nettle's beautiful wings. "You cannot carry me, can you?"

"I do not believe I could fly us both there. I've been feeling… weaker." Nettle looked around her; a bottle on the deck, a flapping sail, the decomposing head of a villager. "Can we not take this vessel?"

"You don't know much about sailing, do you? Do boats in your world have cracked masts, severed backstays, and torn sails?"

"I've floated on poti roots along the river, but I know nothing of sailing. We do not have vessels such as this in Sceanth."

Deflatedly, Kole said, "It doesn't seem as though we have any other option. The ocean's taken every boat of ours away from us." She inspected the boat closer. "It does appear to be in better sailing shape than any of the others rotting on this beach, all things considered." She noted that most of the spare rigging must have been lost at sea. One of the large sails was torn, which would likely be a problem, though not so much if there were some benevolent winds on their side. The water itself was choppy, bigger waves punching into smaller waves, but the real danger lied in Erw's sentient, hostile ocean, and not the actual storm at sea. A torn sail—maybe even two—could get them out to find the island. As long as Nettle was sure of the path, her memory would lead them along.

Still, there remained the virtually insurmountable task of getting the boat back into the water.

When the cries of birds above began—not screeching seabirds, but cawing ravens—so too did the fog begin to dissipate. Unnoticeable at first, but the sea smoke quickly parted, and the night sky was visible once more. There was a glow on the horizon, behind them and beyond grassy hills and the messy tips of the shadowy woods. Beautiful, almost. If Erw's inherent darkness weren't so frightening. Nettle recalled the sun of Sceanth, and how it burned off the morning mist from river stones and killorn trees. She imagined Kole must still remember the light of Erw, before the sun seemed to stop rising altogether.

Something rumbled in the distance. Probably thunder, though Nettle wasn't about to presume anything based on her time in this place. The ocean waves surged, smashing the boats again and sending shivers across the land. Far off, she sensed the fishing village quiver, trembling beneath encroaching waves that were only growing in size.

Nettle was sure the waves held many dark secrets and many creatures of utter mystery, some perhaps still undiscovered by the people of Erw. And she was certain she saw one of them. It surfaced for only a moment, lumbering heavily yet gracefully through the current. Not so unlike what she glimpsed during her experience within the Obsidian Revenant: the greenish, bluish, and grayish glimmering scales along the spine of the gargantuan beast.

And then another rumbling, though she realized it was more of a howl. She knew it was hope.

Kole spotted it in the water too now. "Is that—?"

"The serpent, yes. I believe your hope has finally come." The girls held hands and also took in the unearthly beauty of what was happening.

Impossibly, the fishing trawler began rocking as the water pooled beneath it, like spilled milk seeping beneath floorboards. Air filling desperate lungs. The farther out the tide spread, the more alive the boat became, until it was again fully in the water. The serpent had done its job using the sea to pull and push the trawler back out onto the waves. With massive, clawed hands, the great beast propelled itself back out to sea, to be unseen once more. And once the girls and the boat were away from the beach, they were on their own again.

With a portentous cackle, the ravens flew off somewhere, enveloped by the returning sea smoke.

CHAPTER 18

"LISTEN TO THE THUNDER," KOLE CALLED OVER POUNDING waves. "It lets you know how far out the storm is."

Nettle tried her best to focus. But try as she might, she did not hear thunder. Only an echoing, haunting laughter. It was becoming a constant in her head. Guttural. Unnatural.

"Right now, it is only a distant rumble. My father told me to pay attention to details like that. He taught me everything about sailing." With taut arms, Kole directed the boom as well as she could, difficult considering the many scattered holes and tears in the sails. Splashing seawater hit them both, soaking them in its freezing bitterness. "Still never let me come out with them," she added with some vitriol.

The boat veered sharply and crested the tip of a massive incoming wave. Nettle held tightly to whatever part of the boat was within her reach, while Kole remained indomitable. The girl had a renewed sense of hope after witnessing the great serpent in the waves. "When the waters are rough, it's a good idea to avoid low clouds, too."

"How do you tell the clouds from the sea smoke?" Nettle called out, but she did not receive an answer.

Kole was noticeably adept at piloting even a damaged vessel as this through torrential conditions. Of course, there did seem to be another force guiding them where Nettle directed. It could only have been the serpent, she thought, safeguarding their passage. Over angry waves, Kole continued to reinforce the importance of such things as: "Watch for debris in the water," "Pump out the bilges to keep the boat high," and "Head the bow into waves at forty-five-degree angles." None of it made much sense to the faerie, but Kole had certainly been training herself well.

Still, she did not know where it was in the ocean they were; she was only following the faerie's vague, instinctual directions. She maneuvered the boat between a pair of tall rocky spires jutting out from the surface. At one point, splashing water appeared almost deep purple in color, and bits of slimy black matter stuck to their bodies and clothing. Kole knew nothing of the tall, pointy rocks or the strange black bits from the ocean— no maps she'd ever read described anything of the like; it was a different world out there.

Thankfully, the fury powering the waves soon dwindled. The fishing boat leveled out and loose bottles and other discarded objects on the deck found corners to roll into.

It wasn't until Nettle spotted the lambent blue glow in the distance—faint within the sea smoke at first, but then bright enough to reflect off the water's calming surface—that she knew they were close. Nettle spoke, with a mixture of relief and fear, "That is her."

The silhouette of a figure in a boat materialized within the blue glow. She rowed away serenely from the approaching fishing vessel, though ostensibly unaware of it.

"That is who we must follow," the faerie said.

Kole's posture and muscles relaxed; the ocean's rage having suddenly been reduced to barely a simmer. "She will take us to the island?"

"And to the Obsidian Revenant."

"*Buk-bawk.*"

"I think I am as leery as Talem," Kole spoke. "But I trust you, Nettle. I've trusted you this far. I know not who the woman in the boat might be, but I will place my trust in you."

Their trawler had slowed in the calming waters, yet a current began pushing them in the direction of the smaller boat.

Nettle said, "I saw the same boat the night I discovered the island. Though she did not heed my call. I followed, only to lose her in the sea smoke. But then the island revealed itself to me." She looked at Kole with mercy. "And this is how you and I will find it, too."

Again, Kole repositioned the spar, gripping it tightly with cold, wet hands. The waves were picking up but coming at them from no particular direction. She paid no attention to the water however, strictly focusing on the boat in the growing distance. There was a chill trailing behind it. A dead freezing, like being at the bottom of a well in winter. The woman's long hair blew gently in the breeze. "Who is she?"

"Perhaps a traveler. Perhaps someone who has been here for a long while now."

The distance between the boats was growing, yet Nettle was certain that was how it was meant to work. And Kole was certain of Nettle.

The ocean grew even quieter. Kole swallowed hard. "There is a story told around here; more of a fable, I suppose. About a girl from our village who walked out into the frigid waves and never returned."

"In Sceanth, there really is no difference between fables and stories. We don't tell tales of that which is not real. Of that which didn't happen. Or what *won't* happen." She shook the memories of home from her mind and returned to her place on Erw. Nettle tilted her head, questioning the water surrounding them. The figure in the rowboat had vanished from sight, once again consumed by the gray nothingness. "This girl—? She simply walked out through the waves?"

"As it goes."

"Perhaps it was the lure of the island?"

"Perhaps." Kole stopped for a moment to take note of her own place on Erw. "Or perhaps the island did not exist until she found it? But as far back as my people have talked, they have talked of her. My mother tried to tell the story to me, but I knew she was only piecing it together herself."

"How does her story go?"

"When babies are born in our village, upon their first daybreak, a midwife will bring them here to the ocean. Through the misty morning dew they'll come to the ocean, and the midwife will tie a sprig of cordgrass around the babies' wrists before dipping them into the harsh water."

"You as well?"

"Aye. But this baby…they say there was a seabird that snatched the cordgrass from the girl's arm, and she was doused in the ocean without it. Some have said this was a curse. Some of the more naïve believed the baby's ungodly scream was nothing, really. But then some others were certain it cast a pall over the entire village. It brought storms and ocean tides of malice bent only on destruction. It brought starvation and disease." She winced a little as grim malaise surrounded them. "And eventually, it brought *this*, too."

Kole questioned Nettle about the location of the rowboat, that was now completely out of sight. Nettle only told her to keep heading straight. She was obviously cold, as Kole could see the faerie was shivering and rubbing her hands against the bumps on her rough skin.

"When the child grew up, and she stepped into the malevolent water and disappeared from the village forever, the stories about her only multiplied. Had the seabird taken more than just the cordgrass around her wrist? Was she taken by some unseen force? Was she ever really there? Was she only born to haunt the village?"

Nettle was hanging on to Kole's story, but their boat began rocking enough to snap them both out of it. The unmistakable sound of the ocean's fury, smashing and pulverizing rocky cliffs, could be heard through the darkness. "Hold on," Nettle said. "We are close now."

Her words brought an unexpected assault upon the boat.

One wave hit the starboard side as another collided with the portside. The trawler almost spun, nearly capsized, but Kole kept it in place by looping a length of rope over the mast and securing it tightly to the stern. The rocking made Nettle nauseous, so she released her wings and floated free of the boat. Gale winds blasted, seemingly from nowhere, and Nettle grabbed a flapping sail in desperation, tearing it free from its rigging. She lost sight of Kole in the sea spray and smoke but could hear her calling out to the faerie. Nettle's attention could not be everywhere, however, and another wave knocked the trawler into a cluster of sharp rocks. The hull split. A mast cracked in two.

The ocean continued to take what it could.

What was left of the boat managed to land mercifully on the shore of the hidden island, in a bed of large black stones and long-rotted driftwood. For the faerie and the fisher girl though, the storm was not as charitable. Their bodies hit rocky outcroppings, consciousness pulled and torn from them by foul, creeping hands of ethereal evil.

CHAPTER
19

"GO ON AND DISAPPEAR THEN, LITTLE FAERIE. DISAPPEAR *from Sceanth. But I'll remain here, wishing you never existed in the first place."*

It was the satyr's voice that fluttered through Nettle's mind. Like a flung stone skipping across a lake top; barely touching in places, connecting just enough to leave a mark. It was not a memory, since she did not recall such words being said to her, but maybe more in her imagination? A dream? She was certainly finding it to be more and more difficult to differentiate dreams here. Like dreams, being in Erw was a fluid mixture of good and bad. Suffering and respite.

"Go on and disappear, little faerie."

In her memory, Nettle flew from his woodland den and back to the bluebell fields for the last time. She saw her mother once more, perhaps out of some unconscious hope that she might give Nettle a reason to stay. But Nettle returned to her life vein cocoon nevertheless. Even despite her mother's words: *"There is danger to be found in other worlds, daughter. A darkness that, if in too deep, bluebell fae may not find their way out of."* Cleo warned her: *"Your dreams will only worsen."* Cleo had her daughter check herself, the decisions she'd been making, and the choices she still had an opportunity to make: *"Have you chosen your life veins carefully, Nettle?"*

And still Nettle returned to her cocoon.

One last voice in her head. It was her final conversation with Piper. Sweet Piper, who only wished the best for both of them, and wished for Nettle to end things with the satyr. He had some strange hold over Nettle, one the faerie was only then realizing she still had the power to wriggle out of. She held Piper's quivering hands in her own and begged, *"Will you promise me you'll keep it a secret?"*

"If you promise to end it," Piper said.

There they sat, upon that giant frozen toadstool outside the faerie enchantment and the bluebell fields. Nettle could recall just how much she hoped it wouldn't be the last time they spoke. But something had to end, and she was not certain of what it would be. If a bluebell faerie's fault was to fall in love too easily, surely others before her must have felt similar remorse and guilt? Was Nettle so different from the rest? As much as she herself could feel hurt, she also seemed to know how to hurt others. It was more than just a fault.

It was a curse.

"Promise you'll end it, Nettle."

And curses had a way of following one from place to place. In dreams and in other worlds. Even worlds where one might have hoped to find a greater love.

"Will you promise me?" There was a shift in Nettle's feelings; this no longer felt like a memory, a dream, or an apparition. This felt *real.* Piper had a necklace on, sitting atop those wonderful collarbones. It had tiny, sparkling golden seashells tied to it. Nettle hadn't noticed it before, and thought it peculiar, as shells like these were a rare thing indeed in Sceanth.

"I promise," Nettle finally said.

And with that promise, Piper was no longer Piper. The

gentle faerie's lime green aura melted away, wings folded up into nothing, and her soft features hardened. Her hair turned from lush, sparkling forest green to a wiry, dull gray. There was still beauty in her face, but it was worn-down and nearly forgotten. Her eyes were almost colorless. From behind a once-pointed ear came a voros moth, and it quickly fluttered away somewhere unseen. The seashell necklace remained. "A promise is a promise, little faerie. And certain promises often require taking strong measures."

Nettle did not know who the woman was, nor did she fully understand the meaning of her words.

"Little faerie? Can you make that promise?" The woman touched Nettle's cheek with her cracked fingertips.

"I—I have already given my word." Nettle answered, with some confusion as to what her *own* words meant now.

"An easy enough thing to give. Very few will see a promise all the way to its end." The strange woman drew her eyes toward Nettle's hand, directing the faerie to look for herself. She was holding a wilted white orchid. A thick liquid oozed from its stem. Nettle stuck her tongue to it, but it had no taste or memories to share. "After all he's done to you—for the curse that is your burden—you know what must be done in return."

"Your dreams will only worsen." The words echoed in Nettle's head as she studied the flower in her hand.

Nettle looked back up, but the woman was gone. The orchid, too. Both were no more than black wisps melding with the terrible sea smoke until the fog itself dissipated and nothing was left but a dark forest before her. The sweet smell of cedar brought her back to her senses, and she suddenly remembered the storm and being thrown from the boat, a torn sail clutched tight in her hands. What remained of the sail was a few steps away, past rotting driftwood, flapping from the ocean's biting draft before the jagged maw of the forest. An unsettling howl came from just beyond the outlying trees. She turned her head skyward, but the tallest point of the island—the rocky precipice where the Obsidian Revenant grew—was still partially masked by gray.

The boat must have crashed upon the shore, too. But there was no sign of it. Or of Kole. There were some unusual splashes in the water; they seemed to be borne from more than the tide, like something substantial was struggling beneath, but as closely as she looked, Nettle could see nothing.

An image flashed in her head: that of the single stem of bluebells she'd spotted the last time she was here, growing outside the entrance to the forest. Stepping to the sail, Nettle pulled it away from the ground, revealing the purple bluebells, though they were nowhere as bright as they were before. The flowers were damaged, like an animal of some sort had gnawed at the stem and rent the petals from it. They had no scent either, and Nettle immediately discovered the sensation of missing the abundant fields and flowing rivers in the lands of Sceanth.

She missed Piper, too, and wondered what it might have been about the ocean that ever made her imagine a greater love could be had.

This cursed island was full of ways to make one doubt and hate.

A familiar *buk-buk-bawk* penetrated the muffled static of the black woods. "Talem—?" Nettle trudged through the brush and found the headless chicken tip-tapping his feet on the dirt. Even after the adventure on the boat he still had the bluebell stem from the serpent shrine tied around his neck. "You…you wish for me to follow you?" He flapped his wings excitedly then turned and ran ahead.

Nettle took one more look behind her in the foolish hope that Kole might be right there. Of course she wasn't. And so, Nettle followed the bird into the woods.

"There is danger to be found in other worlds, daughter. A darkness that bluebell fae may not find their way out of."

They walked for only a few minutes, the faerie and the chicken, before coming to a small clearing. No trees grew here; the gloomy woods seemed to avoid the square-shaped patch of long grass. There was dark cover from the canopy above, though a few slashes of moonlight filtered through. Muffled howls continued in the distance. As Nettle slowed to inspect the edge of the clearing, she felt something touch her shoulder, yet there was nothing there. A terrible smell drifted past.

"Why do you not fear things, Nettle?" The echo of words returned to her head. If the satyr could see her here on Erw, he would not be asking such questions. Fear seemed to be a thing that was only multiplied in the realm of Erw. Even for the bravest of faeries and the great beasts which lurked in the ocean's depths.

"Buk buk-awk," Talem clucked from behind, breaking Nettle away from her inner distractions.

And then a heavy drip of something plopped on her shoulder. Through the creaking of tall trees, there was the fuzzy pattering of more hitting the grass. Around her, in the corners of the clearing in the woods where trees lurched like phantasms, and from the sky came a dark, downpour of some horrid, unnatural dread.

Talem had scuttled off somewhere again. As Nettle tried to place the chicken's whereabouts, she spotted a line of sticks leading out of the grass. Not so much a path, but more like a pattern: they were zig-zagging at curious angles and crossing over top and underneath in ways which seemed to be purposeful. The bark had been peeled from the sticks; shaved off with a sharp instrument of some sort. She followed them out of the clearing, sheltered from the ominous storm by the trees' uncertain depths.

Aways in and through some ferns, Nettle found Kole. She was crouched before a rock, inspecting it with her chin resting upon dirty knees. Talem stood a few feet back of the girl; the way his feet were planted made his stance appear suspicious. The rock was more like a large, flat tablet in shape, and it was propped up against a mound of dirt and bark.

"Look at this," Kole spoke softly. She was not baffled or suspicious at all of Nettle's sudden presence.

Nettle crouched too, with one hand on Kole's back. The girl's bones felt sharp and she was cold to the touch, even through her sweater. The rock had a message scratched into it. Three ominous words:

...OBEY POISON WORLDS...

Kole traced the jagged scratch marks which made up the words; letter by letter she ran a dirty finger through them.

"What is their meaning?" Nettle asked.

"I don't know. Poison worlds—? It doesn't make any sense to me."

Nettle noticed a tear in Kole's sweater, and some blood on the back of her neck, presumably damage inflicted after being tossed from the boat herself. She reached her hand out to maybe heal however she could, but Kole rose before Nettle could make contact. "We should keep going," she said abruptly and headed deeper into the shadowy woods. The faerie and the chicken followed.

The woods became ever more dark and damp. The pattering above them continued. For warmth, the girls held onto one another closely; arms entwined, fingers locked. They climbed ever upwards, hoping they would very soon reach the rocky precipice from which the Obsidian Revenant grew. Nettle did not remember flying so high up the first time she found the hidden island but thought perhaps the trek only felt longer because they were on foot, and tired from so much walking through the lands of Erw.

A shiver shot through her. She turned to find Kole staring at her weakly. "Could—could you increase your glow a little? So we might be more comfortable in this place?"

"I have been trying," Nettle said. She held her hand up higher, fingers splayed, but, if anything, her amber-pink glow only grew dimmer.

"It is so dark. Freezing." Kole's eyes were not focusing on anything at all; jittery gray pupils like coffin-flies over fresh carrion.

"I'm sorry. I'm trying. But…I cannot." She wished she could do more. Her power was fading. Nettle knew it was the work of the ocean. The sea smoke. The Erw Witch. Fear bubbled within her. "I'm sorry, Kole."

But Kole was not just cold, not just uncomfortable in the dark; she was no longer moving. She braced herself on a thin, crooked tree; it was bent harshly, as though it only wished to point as far away from the moon and stars as possible.

"Kole—?"

She breathed heavy, concentrated breaths, fighting to take in air. "I do not feel well. Nettle, I—" Kole looked up toward the faerie and her eyes went as black as the woods. Under the light of the moon slipping through the cracks in the trees above, Kole was clearly changing. Nettle didn't move but leaned in a little closer, partly out of fear and partly hoping her glow might still be strong enough to dissolve the dark's deceptions. But there was no hidden hope. Kole's color was dimming, her forehead hardened and cracked. Whatever was happening, it reminded Nettle of the dryads who lived in the Sier Woods of Sceanth. The peaceful Sier dryads who sprouted leaves from their shoulders, branches from their elbows, and grew moss between their fingers. But there was nothing peaceful about Kole's transformation.

Nettle watched in horror, hands to her mouth, unable to move a muscle.

Kole screamed as every tendon and muscle and bone within her turned to earthly wood and pulled apart; branches untwisting like baskets unweaving. Her one hand remained clutched to the tree, even as the rest of her was breaking apart. Her forearm snapped, leaving the wooden hand fused to the bark. She screamed one final, torturous roar, but even her voice changed, sounding more like the creaking bend of a tall tree in a mighty windstorm. For only an instant, her eyes flared a haunting, fiery blue before her body split, snapped, and crumbled.

Until all that was left of the fisher girl was a small pile of sticks on the ground.

Nettle flew quickly over to the remains. "Kole!" The sticks burned to the touch, and Nettle pulled away. More than anything, she only wished to be closer, but could do no more than move farther away from the senseless eradication of her friend.

She stepped back to the company of Talem; the chicken remained waiting a safe distance away. The faerie cried sorrowful tears into Talem's feathers.

There was the echo of a dying wind and the creaking of the woods around her. The howling of far-off critters. The sense of wicked spirits imperceptibly passing through.

The broken hand still clung to the crooked tree like a ghastly branch.

A sensation came over Nettle, and just like the dreams experienced within her cocoon, there was a moment when she knew for certain none of this was real. That this was just one more poisoned world, and it was only in her head. All she had to do was wake up.

Again, her mother's words rang in her head: *"Have you chosen your life veins carefully, Nettle?"*

CHAPTER
20

echoed in her head over and over, until it slowly faded to nothing. The darkness folded away, too, until it was clear Nettle was back on the island's rocky shore. The tide was lapping hungrily across her body, but she was far beyond being bothered by the water's freezing grasp.

A howl from the ocean brought another surge of tide in with it, and the waves washed over Nettle, again and again. She shook her head clear then noticed Kole on the shore, too, just out of arms' reach. Kole winced in sudden pain, clutching her leg.

"What is it?" Nettle asked, lurching over to her side.

"Something…something in the water. Bit me, I think." The tide momentarily descended back out to the ocean, taking some of the girl's blood out with it. Stuck to her calf was a tentacled, fist-sized, gelatinous sea creature. "Ah! It burns," she cringed.

Kneeling beside her now, Nettle reached over and put a palm to the rust-colored jellyfish; its voice was faint, but she knew it wanted to be separated from Kole as much as Kole wished for the thing to be free from her. It pulsated a little under Nettle's hand, and in a silent moment of shared empathy, their combined luminescent energies flared weakly, before the jellyfish disengaged itself from the girl and floated back into the shallow depths of the tide. Kole bent over even more. Blood was pouring from her wound.

"It hurts," she said through gritted teeth. "The water stings!"

Nettle pressed a dimly-glowing hand to Kole's leg; straining, for her magicks were certainly fading. It took everything she had but it was still not enough. The girl's wound was not healing.

Kole didn't have to say a word; she pleaded with her big eyes, once gray, but now sparkling preternaturally. "I'm sorry," the faerie spoke quietly, helplessly. "I don't know if there is any more I can do. I—" For a moment, she replayed the dream she'd just experienced in her mind: how she watched helplessly as Kole turned to wood and withered into nothing. But Nettle stopped. She released her blood-sopping hands from Kole and took the girl's hands into her own. Kole's clenched fists relaxed, and Nettle brought them to the leg wound. Astoundingly, a dim but wonderful amber-pink glow emanated from Kole's hands. Her entire body flared enough to cast a warmth between them.

"What…is…happening?" Kole asked. Ignoring the pain in her leg, she brought both hands in front of her to inspect them. "How am I doing this?"

"You have healed yourself when I could not. Look." Nettle wiped the blood from Kole's leg, and the wound was no longer there.

"Your gift—" Kole muttered, mostly just to herself. She studied her hands even closer—the backs of them, her palms, and back again—perhaps not fully convinced of the wonder that was occuring. "This is the gift you gave me, is it not? When we kissed at the shrine." It was difficult for Kole to take her eyes off her own body.

The faerie washed the blood off her hand into the ocean, which lapped it up vehemently. "I think so, yes."

"I mean, I've felt this glow, but I thought it was from being around your *own* light, Nettle. And now, I just healed myself from a jellyfish sting. I made the cocoon back in the tree above the serpent shrine, didn't I? That was *me*, was it not?"

But the faerie had no answer.

"And these terrible visions I've been seeing—? You said you'd given me your dreams, too. I am becoming just like you. Aren't I?"

Nettle's response was quiet, like she was ashamed of her own answer. "Not like me. Like I *was*, Kole. The gifts you are gaining are merely the same ones I am now losing." Nettle touched her sharp fingers to Kole's skin. It felt much different—more fantastic—than it did a moment ago; more like the enchanted fields in Sceanth and less like the dark realm of Erw. And Nettle was not oblivious to the fact that the girls' dreams were becoming shared experiences, too. Just as many bluebell faeries' do. "But it seems that way, yes. As I said before, it can be difficult to tell what it is the gift will lead to. Or how the tithe will be resolved."

Kole's dim glow disappeared completely. "The *tithe*—? What does that mean?"

With darting eyes, Nettle searched around them. The sea smoke was at a distance but still all around them, almost like a large dome. Nettle searched as far as she could along the shore and across the ocean. She sensed Agatha back in Sceanth, beneath the sacred white alder tree, still teaching more young fae about tithes; warning them of dangers, while smiling to herself because of details she did not wish to share. "I will tell you in time, Kole. Not now." The water clawed at their legs furiously; if it could, it would have gripped them both and pulled them under.

"What time do we *have*, Nettle? Are these dark dreams part of it, too? These hallucinations that won't let me go? Never have I experienced such torment." Kole reached out and touched Nettle's cheek softly, to be certain the faerie was really with her. "Just now, before this jellyfish sting, I saw you *die*! You turned into sticks, and you vanished before my eyes."

Exactly as Nettle had witnessed, only she had envisioned Kole perish instead. The girl's description was the same. "But

I didn't die. I'm right here." Was it possible for the Erw Witch's power to seep into their consciousness, poisoning their own thoughts and their very dreams? Hallucinations might be closer to the truth, just as Kole had said. The sea smoke may have been feeding off creatures' wants and fears. "We're both right here."

"Are we?"

"Once, I feared nothing more than *not* having my dreams. Escape within my life vein cocoon was all I had. And more than anything, I wished to find the ocean. Now, here on Erw, my dreams feel more real than anything else. But perhaps this is because I no longer know if I am truly awake? Perhaps I'm not. And perhaps it no longer matters?" She looked up, somewhere in the direction of the island's peak. "Can you tell me what else you saw in your dreams just now?"

Kole took one more look at her leg, the rising tide masking where the creature pierced her skin, and she wondered if maybe the wound was a dark hallucination, too. "I saw a…creature. He held a torch in his hands, and he was burning a monstrous tree to nearly nothing. Each pop of flame and every snap and crack of wood pained me, as though the tree was a part of me. Or myself, a part of it." She paused to remember the flitting details. "And when I looked at myself in the dream, I found my own arms ablaze. They were nothing more than horrible plumes of black smoke." Kole hugged herself in an attempt to shed her body of the thought. "I saw my mother, too. She asked me to promise her something. It was just like one of the last times I saw her. Before she was taken by the ocean, too." Still, Kole managed a sliver of a smile. "What's funny is, she used to call me 'Little Faerie'. That was her nickname for me."

The ocean waves became ugly and twisted. Like a pit of snakes. Unnatural.

And Nettle recollected her own vision on the island. Her memory of Piper, which morphed into a woman Nettle did not recognize. The woman said, *"A promise is a promise, little faerie. And certain promises often require taking strong measures."* Did Kole see her, too? Nettle asked, "What was the promise you made?"

Kole was holding something back. What it was—whether the truth or half-truth or some guilty admission—Nettle did not know. "It's not something I can say, Nettle. But she transformed into a faerie, like she had a glamour of her own, maybe?"

"Did she glow a sublime green, this faerie?"

"Aye. She was nearly as beautiful as you."

Nettle hesitated, thinking of Piper as best she could. "I am finding it difficult myself to remember those I've loved." She pulled the photograph from out of her dress and unfolded it. Kole and her parents. Her mother wore a necklace of seashells, even in the black and white picture the adornment sparkled like gold. She held it out for Kole. "I found this in your home. And I kept it. I'm sorry."

For a moment, Kole's emotions boiled within her as she looked upon the familiar photograph. It was creased and torn and wet and stained from the saltwater. But she was quick to fold it back up. "You saw her too, didn't you?"

"I believe so. Though I also believe the reasons for these shared dreams of ours go far beyond the gift you were given at the serpent shrine." Kole questioned Nettle with a tilt of her head. With a shaky hand, the faerie pointed upwards to where the jagged rock face looked out above the treetops. "The Erw Witch. She is up *there*."

Kole's eyes followed where the faerie cast her hand.

"I saw *you* die, Kole. Just as you saw *me*. Transformed into sticks. And *she* has seen it all, too." The ravens could be heard in the distance, hidden somewhere in the clouds above; Nettle knew they were watching. She pointed a finger to the sky now. "The witch's eyes fly above us," she said.

"You know something I do not, Nettle?"

Nettle took a moment to taste the saltwater on the back of her hand and then spat it out. "She spoke to me from within the tree."

"What did she speak of?"

"She spoke of the ocean. Of the serpent. And of lost memories."

"The lost memories of oceans?"

"Precisely."

"Just as my mother used to say, also." Kole collected bits from her memory and pieced them together. "She would tell me, *'There's no better place to be forgotten than in the lost memories of oceans.'*"

"Do you suppose…your mother has some connection to this witch? Could she—?"

Kole huffed a tiny laugh. "Not my mother, no. All she's known has been our village. Books have told me that witches are typically born from witches. Or from one witch and one human. But the stories I've overheard—mostly from frightened townsfolk in Yarari—tell of the Erw Witch having come from no one. Maybe from a place instead."

The dome of sea smoke was closing in on them, becoming smaller. All the while, the ocean's waves were growing larger. The girls were mindful of the changes, and Nettle reached out an open hand for Kole, hoping they might take their conversation elsewhere. "I fear it is no longer safe here with the tides, Kole. Let us make our way to the island's peak."

"It will be no safer up there, Nettle." The girl tried to make her own flare, to bring the glow back, but nothing happened. "I…I'm not sure I'm strong enough."

"You cannot run from this, Kole. You cannot avoid what it is you *fear*. Just as I once did. If I've learned anything here on Erw, it is just that." Nettle's open hand remained extended for the girl to take. "If the witch's power can keep the serpent away any longer, she'll destroy everything, won't she?"

Kole remained in place. Her tears dripped from her chin into the sand. "Has she not already?"

"Not everything. And because I've passed my gifts to you, you can no longer choose the paths I once did. You are stronger than I ever was. Think about what it is you love, Kole. And fight for it."

The girl wiped the tears from her face. It was clear she was hesitating, either because of the things she loved or due to the demons which haunted her.

"Trust in my promises," Nettle said. The bitter wind tugged

at her weathered dress. "And trust in the hope you've always kept with you. It is the purpose of the serpent, is it not?"

The ravens continued to circle them from above. "Those birds, though. Should we be worried that she can see what we're doing?"

"She sees everything. There's no sense fearing what it is she knows."

Kole tried her flare once more and was again met with nothing. Certainly though, she still *felt* different. "What *should* we fear?"

The faerie pressed her lips together; she did not pretend she had the right answer for Kole. She merely said, "Everything. And nothing." Then Nettle walked ahead as thunder rolled heavily in the far distance, black and white ravens dissolved in and out of the sea smoke and hopes and fears of auspicious faerie gifts hung invisible in the air.

Walking along the beach, Nettle drew lines in the opaque mist surrounding her. She drew an orchid from her memory, and it hung in place for a moment before the sea smoke sealed itself back up. As the girls carried on, she drew more shapes: ocean waves, a serpent, a childlike heart, and the outline of a five-winged voros moth. The imagery made her smile a little, which was enough for now.

The Erw Witch's magicks were palpable. The girls followed a path through the sea smoke—a tunnel almost—that opened before them and closed behind them as they moved along. Their hands remained locked together. Nettle carved lines in the mist while Kole's thoughts were placed somewhere unexplained though clearly specific.

They came to a cluster of trees. Burnt red bark came away from them like half-peeled husks of corn, and their leaves were the same black, hand-shaped leaves the girls had seen in the dead woods.

In the trees there was something inherently sinister. Baiting them. Luring them closer.

Some mushrooms littered a grassy patch before the woods. They were few in number, but a fantastic sight: a kind of bright blue, that Nettle had not witnessed since Sceanth, with tiny white spikes around the tips. A few were covered by the black hands of fallen leaves, wet and clingy from the ocean spray.

One mushroom—more rotted than the rest—was adorned with something else: a few thin tree roots were tied together into the shape of a tiny crown. The crown sat a little crooked and it appeared most whimsical atop the little blue mushroom.

Kole crouched and tapped the crown with the point of her finger. "What is its purpose?"

"I am unsure." Nettle was immediately reminded of the beautiful crowns Piper would weave from golden alder wire. She kissed Nettle every time she placed a newly woven crown atop her head. Those were the most wonderful kisses they ever shared. She shook her head to rid her mind of these thoughts of Piper, memories that were returning so unfairly.

And as she did so, there was a deathly, creaking echo before them. The trees were bending in unnatural ways, pulling themselves apart and opening themselves up for the girls. In an instant, there was a pathway into the dark woods.

Nettle and Kole stood in silence for some time without pulling their eyes from the entrance into the woods. Eventually Nettle asked, "She wants us here, doesn't she? And she wants us to find *her*, too." Kole's hand quivered within Nettle's. She tried to break free, but Nettle held on tighter. "Kole, we *must* do this."

"Is there no other way?"

"At this point, we have no choice. I have no choice."

"What binds you to this undertaking, Nettle?"

"The tithe, I believe."

A power reached out for them; it writhed palpably in the misty air. Nettle let go of Kole and reached her hands out toward the black opening into the woods. The very trees emanated whispers of darkness containing words that could not be made out.

"For a bluebell faerie, to give a gift is to also pay a tithe. Sometimes it's a transformation of some sort. An exile to a world such as this. I was unsure before, but now I know what it is that I must pay." Finally, Nettle stepped beyond the edge of the woods. "I am charged with taking a life. And I will take *hers*."

She spoke with a level of gravity Kole had not heard before. Kole grasped her hand—softer now than it had ever been—and stepped into the darkness.

Reverberating off ocean waves and thick clouds was the bellowing of something prodigious. It was almost certainly the great serpent—still crying out, still trying to help, still latching on to what dwindling hope it could find.

But it sounded more like death now.

Some time passed. Their footsteps became more hurried. More certain. Kole turned to Nettle and asked, "What do you suppose this circle of events really is?"

"The cycle of Erw?"

"Yes. My mother had spoken of it in passing—some legends her own mother had likely passed down to her—and Eamonn did, too. The ocean takes, the serpent returns, the witch responds, and she is eventually destroyed. Eamonn said it was all inevitable. And it continues over and over. What I don't understand is: how does it begin again?" The lingering sea smoke seemed to breathe in, as though pleased with the subject the girl was breaching.

Nettle did not have a response, however. She breathed in just as her surroundings did.

"At what point does its true beginning lay? And how does the witch return upon her being destroyed? Is she reborn as the same? Replaced by another?"

"Kole—" Nettle started and then paused for an extended moment. "There are magicks that simply cannot be explained so easily. Some choose to accept them, some choose to not understand. Others feign any knowledge of them altogether."

"I don't think that helps, Nettle."

"It was not meant to." Nettle thought again of the elder fae Agatha, and how she would explain the bluebells' world to the young ones. "Every world and every soul and every dream within them all are connected. The ocean and the serpent. The bluebell fields of Sceanth and this dark realm of Erw. You and I. But none of it can be explained, not really. Sometimes answers will not come as easily as acceptance. All we can do is choose our life veins carefully." *Choose them wisely*, her mother Cleo would say. *And they, too, will choose the right path for you.*

Kole wiped an eye with the back of her hand. "I still do not understand the life vein stuff, Nettle."

"In time," she smiled, just as both her mother and Agatha once smiled at her. "In time you will."

Kole thought some more. "Have you chosen yours correctly?"

"I believe I have, yes."

There was another recent change in Nettle, one that so far had seemingly gone unnoticed by the bluebell faerie. Not so by Kole. She didn't wish to say it; she did not know *how* to say it. But Kole had noticed since looking back at her while on the boat that Nettle's eyes were not only beginning to lose their iridescence, but they were turning peculiar colors. They were now both blue, but one was the dark dark blue of a clear night sky while the other more like icy frost.

As Nettle glanced back from the trees though, Kole saw them differently: one of black and one of white.

CHAPTER
21

While most considered the Erw Witch to be hideous and grotesque, she did not see herself as such. Sure, she was once unquestionably beautiful, but that felt like a lifetime ago to her. A lifetime can change anyone in many undesired ways. The Erw Witch's life began like the lives of most other witches. Firstly, she was not always a witch. She came from a lush land of rivers and forests. She had a man she tried to love as best she could. And though the first words her man chose every morning were words that explicitly described her beauty, she still felt a pull on her heart from somewhere unseen. Every morning they woke together, she took in the sounds of chirping birds and buzzing wings, as well as the scents of seasonal blooms and fresh dew upon the breeze.

The mornings with her man were sweet enough, but it was her dreams which felt sweetest. Her dreams were where she truly lived.

She often left her man's home to explore the forests and the hills but typically found her adventures overly mundane. Far too expected. Her dreams held so many pleasantly unforeseen worlds to explore, and though she might have sometimes been made to feel ashamed of her dreams—whether wondrous or frightening— she remembered how they mostly empowered her. Once, when she returned from a particularly unsettling dream, her man suggested that perhaps, like most dreams, some of the details might have actually been forgotten; maybe she was only remembering the frightening parts? Maybe the wondrous bits were repressed. Hidden away somewhere. But to his own admission, her man did not experience dreams of any sort, so his suggestions were unfounded. Truthfully, he did not really understand the dreams of others.

He asked her, "Your dreams are not a concrete thing, so what are they, really?"

"They are an escape," she would answer him.

"Escape from what?"

"Possibly everything."

"You cannot leave everything behind though. Impossible! Mightn't you escape into a dream and still take *something* with you?" He spoke partly in riddles but knew of her burgeoning spellcasting: her simple tricks of bent light and disguise were common in any of her circle's gatherings. "Surely you must have a trick you are capable of trying." There was a tinge of jealousy in his mentioning of her expanding abilities.

She considered his suggestion at length, and one night she decided it was worth a try.

She picked through her man's belongings: his books and his tools and his kitchen utensils. He had a low shelf of drinking cups and other such vessels, and she settled on one. Using a concealment spell she'd been secretly practicing, she held the cup within an unreal plane even as she drifted off into one last dream.

She woke in a darkened, musty room. She unveiled the cup, pleased that it had made the journey with her. Bringing the cup down upon a sticky barrel, she placed it hard enough that the noise frightened a rat and it scurried out from underneath. She caught the rodent with a quick hand and studied it for a moment before tasting it. The rat was nothing more than blood and rot and bones, hostility and pestilence. It told her nothing of this place.

Taking the cup back into her hand, she crept up a short stone staircase towards a door. Soft light emanated from the other side. She turned the handle carefully and slowly pushed the creaking, wooden door open, stepping out into an empty tavern. The smell of drink was pungent, but it did not appear as though anyone had been around for a while. And she continued to hold the cup in her hands, afraid that if she put it down again, she might wake up.

The Erw Witch explored the crooked, crumbling town she'd found herself in. Just like any dream, she was amazed by the sights she'd never experienced before, like the iron gas lamps and the few shops full of beautiful clothes and books. There were a few townspeople about, and eventually, she met a girl of her own age, and they quickly became friends. They left the town together, exploring new forests and new hills. The girl was fascinated by her. She asked about the cup in this stranger's hands, to which she was told: "It is nothing."

"It seems important to you," the girl prodded.

The Erw Witch clutched it tighter. "It is the thing that keeps me here. My tether. My anchor. Surely you must also be bound by something of importance."

"If I am, I have not yet found it."

"What about love? There is nothing more important than love. It took me a lifetime to learn this." She breathed in the memory of her man, what she could of it, for it had already been fading fast from her mind. There were others, too, who were becoming just as difficult to recall.

The girl took her hand. The sunlight danced off the necklace she wore, one of sparkling golden seashells. It was juxtaposed by the sadness in her dim, gray eyes. "Will you show me?"

"I can try."

The girl snickered. "*A lifetime*, you say? You are as young as me, silly."

"I will tell you what *my* mother once told me: *Our dreams will inevitably age us. We can only hope we might choose the right ones.*"

Eventually, they came to a sandy shore. The more time she spent in this place, the more questions she had: questions about the ocean and why she felt drawn to it and why the people feared its power. The girl told her about the great serpent, an unseen monster beneath the tide. She had been taught the serpent was nothing more than a story, not a thing worth wasting her time believing in. But in her heart, the girl knew the serpent was real. The girl talked much about Erw's sentient ocean, how it knew only of destruction of the shores. And how the serpent was charged with bringing hope back to the people, driving the furious tides away. Over and over. *A cycle*, the girl had called it. *An unbroken circle.*

The Erw Witch grew ever more curious about these local superstitions. "And how might the circle *become* broken?"

And as she asked this, there was a thick fog that moved in. It had come from a faraway place. It seeped through peaty moors, dying forests, and marshy bogs. The fog had followed the girls all the way to the shore. In a way, it was erasing everything behind them. Destroying the path they'd carved through their journeys across Erw.

"There is a witch," the girl whispered. "She dwells within the shambliest of shacks nestled upon the highest of rocks in Erw. Her presence is obscured partly by blackened trees and tall, browning grass, but mostly by nightmares and the visiting souls from other worlds. She is death in life and life in death. She is the lost memories of oceans."

"A witch—?" And her words were drawn out as she considered the concept of such a creature. For she had not heard that word used quite the same before. The fog crept ever further into her subconscious, permeating her very soul. She wanted to know more.

"Aye. And she aims to break the cycle by taking away any hope we have." The girl scanned the ocean, looking out as far as she could. "This sea smoke that surrounds us now…this is her. There's something sinister about it—a different kind of evil than the ocean itself—that is keeping the serpent at bay and allowing the ocean to take what it wishes."

She couldn't help it, but the Erw Witch smirked a little to herself as the girl told her tale.

"To destroy the witch is to continue the cycle. It *must* be done. But I fear the witch can no longer be destroyed. She has grown too powerful to be killed." The girl twisted her seashell necklace around her fingers. "And all we are left with now is hope."

The Erw Witch stopped for a moment and considered this girl in her company. She felt the urge to pass a part of herself onto the girl. A gift of sorts. She reached down to her feet and took some of the cold dirt into her hands, squeezing it tight, out through the cracks between her fingers.

But she stopped.

For reasons she wasn't sure of, she released the dirt, sprinkling it back onto the ground. Whatever it was she thought she might have given the girl, in that moment she chose not to.

Instead, she told the girl she would find this witch. She would go into the sea's smoke and follow it to the witch's home. And she would destroy her. The girl smiled at the foolish display of bravado. Still, she knew there was something special about this stranger she'd grown close to. She asked, "How can I be certain of your return?"

The Erw Witch held out the cup that was still in her possession. "I'll give this to you. Surely I will need to return to my anchor, won't I?"

The girl smiled knowing in her heart that whatever promises were being made, they were being made just for her. And she asked her to stay one more night and leave in the morning, but the Erw Witch left immediately, with only one last kiss.

It was a long and lonely journey through the sea smoke. The farther she went, the more it felt as though she belonged at its end. The dread persisted too, but she had no choice, as though she was forcibly being pulled closer to her destination. In time, and after much searching, she came to that highest point in Erw: a rocky precipice where the sea smoke thinned enough to view the night sky full of speckled stars above, while also overlooking the swirling gray mist below. A sea of dreadful oblivion. Shapes appeared and reappeared in the misty nothingness: waves and serpents and morphing faces of those she'd known, those she'd forgotten, and those she had yet to meet. Sinister mouths cackled her name and called out words she could not comprehend.

But she also found she was beginning to gain control of the sea smoke. It had filled the depths of her and become a part of her. It listened to her, and it waited for something more.

And there was a massive tree. Double the size of any she'd ever known. It was pitch black—as dark as the most hidden cave—its roots grew all over the rocky surroundings, and the tree's thick branches reached straight up, stretching into the celestial night as far as they could.

The tree was in her head, whispering secrets of the world to her she did not yet understand.

Not yet.

Beyond the black tree was a house. More a rotting shack than a warm home. Smoke streamed from the jagged tip of a crumbling chimney, jutting out from a mossy roof. There were no windows, and the door was nothing more than a stained, frayed cloth hanging from the top of the frame. The wind that blew across the top-most tip of Erw did not ruffle the cloth at all. A warm glow filled the inside of the shack.

She peered through the space between the cloth and the doorframe.

"Welcome," came a woman's voice. Her words cut through the air in a graceless fashion, like a rusty cleaver through a thick carcass.

"Who are you?"

The woman wore ill-fitting rags, too big and too small at the same time. She had a threadbare scarf twisted around her neck. Her spotted scalp was visible, and what remained of her hair was wispy and gray, like the last sickly breath expunged from a dying soul. She had one eye of deep green and one that was missing entirely. "I am not what you think. WHO ARE YOU is the real question." The woman's one gaping eye socket still watched on disagreeably.

"I am not of this world."

"None of us are."

"Us—?"

The woman scratched her hairy chin and one of her fingernails broke off. "Witches."

"But I am not a—"

"You are the Erw Witch. As am I."

She remembered her promise to the girl to destroy the witch and had an inkling of a suspicion that her actions here were anticipated. "And I have come here to take your place?" The sea smoke nudged the girl deeper into the room, though the mist had been controlled by the intentions of both women.

"Precisely."

And the sea smoke filled the shack until a darkness not known for a lifetime was born again.

And when it cleared, only a single Erw Witch remained.

The black tree outside the shack had grown a little bit taller.

And one more memory fueled the ocean's fury.

As a witch, she used her newfound spells to leave memories of her old self behind in various corners of Erw. She imbued river stones with the smell and taste of juniper and elderberry. She wove tiny crowns from wiry tree roots, which she would place upon withered and rotting mushrooms. She left tiny sandcastles on beaches and grew a single bluebell on the rocky shore of a hidden island.

But never did she try to grow a cocoon; remembering dreams was one thing but returning to dreams was something else entirely more fearful.

To anyone who crossed her path, she most certainly appeared hideous and grotesque. Not unlike the Erw Witch who had previously lived in the shack upon the highest of rocks in the land. She did not find that she missed her glow or her luminescent wings at all, but she did miss the memory of her mother's parting words. She wished she could recall what they were—what they spoke about that one final time—but the words were simply gone.

From time to time, in moments of weakness, or when she questioned the very tasks she had burdened herself with, she returned to the cellar from which she first emerged. Sometimes it was a difficult space to find, but often, it was a simple enough task to slip back in. Frightening the drunken inhabitants of the tavern at the top of the stairs would often be enough to invigorate the Erw Witch and seize control over the sea smoke again.

Once, when bursting through the cellar door and scuttling out into the street, the Erw Witch stopped when she caught a glimpse of her reflection in the warped glass of the window. Her eyes had changed: one black and one white now, where once they were an iridescent bluish green. She was momentarily confounded—but only momentarily—and then proceeded to pull the orbs from their sockets and tossed them high into the sky, transforming them into ravens.

Across the realm of Erw, in a fishing village on the shores of the furious ocean, a woman placed a framed photograph on the mantle above her hearth. Her husband was out at sea, her daughter off somewhere in the woods. Perhaps at the shrine again. The woman took an extra moment for herself and looked into her own dim eyes in the photograph. There was something else missing in them that she could no longer place. Something she used to know.

She shifted the picture a little closer to a relic on the mantle: a worn copper cup topped with a lid that had a small serpent statue. She removed the lid and looked inside the cup, breathing in the memory of a lost love.

Outside her window, the sea smoke paused momentarily, before rolling along once more.

CHAPTER 22

IT FELT LIKE THEY HAD BEEN IN A DREAM. THE WALK WAS tedious, all the way from the mushroom beach to the highest point in Erw. It was exhausting. But to Nettle and Kole it felt as though it had not taken long at all. Like the way time passes in dreams.

The sea smoke was thinning, but they could not feel its pull any less. The trees had changed along the way, from the peeling trees with black leaves on the beach, to thin, mossy pines, and to great firs with trunks so large it seemed impossible that the hills could support them. And finally, dwarfing even the firs, was the Obsidian Revenant. So immense in stature, it was difficult to comprehend its existence even when its presence there was mostly expected.

The Obsidian roots grew haphazardly across the cold rocks and brown grass. Strange how they seemed to want to grasp what was above ground, rather than beneath it, but there was nothing altogether natural about this black tree. Not the way it grew perfectly straight, not how it absorbed life's light around itself, not how it whispered secrets into one's very soul.

Nettle stepped to the rocky precipice, where she could see the sea smoke receding back down to the ocean and the stars above, the ones not dimmed by the presence of the Obsidian Revenant, that is. She imagined again carving shapes into the fog with her fingers—fingers which were profoundly more rounded and softer than she'd ever known. If only she could reach it, she thought, and she visualized drawing shapes like cloths full of wishes tied to clootie trees, crowns woven from long and twisted branches, and even faerie wings, like the ones she had not unfolded for some time now.

And in the moment before Kole tugged at her arm to get her attention, Nettle could feel herself pulling the swirling sea of gray back closer. She listened for what the smoke wanted, and very nearly whispered what it was *she* wanted from it.

But Kole persisted. "Nettle—?" And the mist's sudden rejuvenation once again ebbed.

Nettle turned to Kole and saw what had sparked the girl. It was a house of sorts. Just past the massive black tree. It had no windows and nothing but a lifeless ragged cloth for a door. There was an intense scent of elderberry in the air. Juniper, too. So strong they seemed to be covering up the stink of something sinister. Death or some rotting thing or another. Wisps of smoke from the chimney trickled in between the stars above. A warm light threaded through the ominous crack between the cloth and the wall.

They approached tentatively and peered through the opening.

A woman sat at a table in the middle of the room. She stoked the fire with a poker in one hand and held a large cup in the other. She wore a dirty white gown, so filthy she appeared to almost be no more than a head and hands in the darkness. Her eyes were absent—two dark pits into nowhere—but two familiar ravens were perched upon the crooked tip of her chair. Across the room there was another small table. Piled on top of it were the many cloth pouches, wet and blackened from their contents.

"Welcome," she said to the prying eyes outside her home. "Come inside, please. Do not hide your intention here." Her voice sounded like bones breaking. It was the fury of the ocean. The shrill wail from the girls' recent memories.

They peeled the cloth back and entered the dwelling.

"Who are you?" Kole asked bluntly.

"Come now. That is a question you have no need of asking." The woman took a long sip from her cup. Both girls recognized the goblet and its worn, dullened hazelnut color. The both recognized it for different reasons. For the cup had traveled from the deceptive hands of the satyr in Sceanth to the dusty mantle above the hearth in the nameless fishing village. Once filled with drunken acrimony and eventually topped with a copper serpent idol. "I am the Erw Witch." She pointed the iron poker directly at Nettle; its point still orange-hot. "As are *you*." It was clear now the object in the woman's hands was not actually a fire poker, but a harpoon instead. Likely pilfered from a fishing vessel.

Nettle's eyes widened. Without her glow she felt like shadowy truths were more difficult to uncover. It was harder to spot a lie in the darkness. Still, she remained unmoved and carefully weighed the usefulness in asking any questions at all.

The Erw Witch spat across the room, her bubbling sputum singed the wooden floorboards at the girls' feet. "I know you did not come here to learn that fact, bluebell faerie. You already know the WHAT. You've come to my home in order to learn the WHY."

"The why means nothing to me, witch."

Her formless eyebrows raised. "Oh? Nothing, you say?" She poked at the fire once more. A burst of flame slashed back at her, missing by inches. The witch swatted it away like it was nothing more than an errant mosquito. "Tell me the truth then. Show me."

Nettle turned to Kole. The fisher girl who was glowing softly, who knew not of what was actually happening. Of what Nettle was truly becoming.

Seeking confirmation with the witch across the room, Nettle asked, "I am...you?" Branches from trees nowhere near the house outside scraped across the roof above them.

The Erw Witch shook her head to say no; her shadowy eyes a black nothingness; her face became more ghostly and ethereal as it swayed back and forth. "No," she said superciliously. "You are *me*." The fire engulfed itself momentarily, making the room black but for the amber-pink glow at the door. And then it flared up again, a thick tongue of flame, hissing and popping. "I was her before me, and she herself was, too."

Kole turned to Nettle and asked, "What is she talking about?"

"It is the life veins," Nettle answered, not taking her eyes off the witch across the room.

The old woman placed the cup down upon the table and scratched at her chin. "Life veins—? I recall the words. Tell me what they mean."

Nettle was unsure whether the witch was playing games, or if she truly did not recognize the details. "A bluebell faerie enters their second phase and creates their cocoon. Inside, they will choose a life vein. For some there are many to choose from. For some, only a few. But they may only choose a *single* life vein. And then the faerie wakes. After emerging from their cocoons, they dissolve them in juni water, and enter their third phase."

Kole considered the words she was hearing. They were words she had heard in bits and scraps before, but never strewn together so precisely.

"Ah," the witch said, remembering. "But some keep their cocoons, do they not?"

The extended silence was ultimately met with Nettle's answer: "Some do."

"Yes. *Some*." With indifference, the witch tossed the harpoon deep into the fire. She placed her withered palms upon the arms of the chair and leaned towards her visitors. "They hide them above the trees and beneath the flora. In ruinous woods no other faerie would dare flutter through." Her mouth was a near-toothless void. "Don't they?"

Nettle hesitated. But then repeated, "Some."

"Your mother's last words. Do you remember them?"

Nettle nodded.

The witch nearly jumped from her chair. The ravens flew from their twin perches onto the edge of the table. "Tell them to me!" She begged like a child who might demand a treat in exchange for nothing. "Please—?"

Nettle wiped the fog from a memory that was already fading. She and her mother were just outside the faerie enchantment, at the stream which trickled slowly in the freezing chill of Winter. It was the final time she saw her mother, before heading back to the satyr woods for one more dream. "She told me to destroy my life vein cocoon."

"Before it destroys you?"

"Yes."

The witch removed herself from her chair now. She hobbled a little closer to the girls, but stopped to place one hand on the back of the black raven. "Has it done so?"

"It is trying to," Nettle said with a tight jaw. "It is certainly trying to."

"Will you let it?" She asked eagerly, taking another unsteady step closer.

Kole tugged on the faerie's sleeve. "Nettle—?"

The Erw Witch sneered at Kole with a crooked finger upon her lips.

But Kole had too many questions. "Nettle, what is she—?"

"Shut this foul thing up!" The witch clenched one hand into a fist, and the floorboards beneath Kole burst open. Dozens of grasping vines wrapped around Kole; coiling around her limbs and over her face. She attempted flaring her glow in defense, like she'd seen Nettle do before, but it was futile. Thorns punctured her skin and with a vine in her mouth, she screamed a terrible, muffled scream.

Nettle did not turn to the girl—how it pained her to not look—but instead kept her gaze upon the Erw Witch.

"I asked, will you let your life vein cocoon consume you for good? Will you let its dreams destroy you?"

"I will not."

Within the vines, Kole's glow increased. The witch took notice. "You have gifted her, I see? An impetuous move, young one." Glimmering light pulsated from Kole's hands, only to fade away and burst from the world like bubbles popping. "But no matter. I have learned to not be so ardent. What's mine is mine." She clenched her fist tighter and Kole went limp, collapsing to the broken floor into growing pools of shimmering blood.

"Leave her be!" Nettle shouted. "Did you not say she was part of the circle? When you pulled me from my dreams at the serpent shrine: you told me the circle would be broken without her."

"You were told about gifting humans, were you not? The woman said as much—the one beneath the white alder tree."

"Agatha? How do you—?"

In one soundless, graceful motion, the ravens sailed from the table's edge to the shoulders of the Erw Witch. She raised her open palms above her head and squirmed her fingers as though scratching at an invisible surface. "The dreams you've had are the dreams of me. The life you lived was mine also. Your time on Sceanth. The bluebell fields. The satyr's woods." She gestured toward the worn cup on the table behind her. "And each time you dreamt of the realm of Erw you entered this world from a different point on the circle. But it is chaotic magick of sorts, for I myself dreamt one last time after you, yet I entered this dark place before." Lowering her hands, she held them out before her, palms aimed at the rickety floor. Each raven fluttered onto the back of a different hand. "The faerie destroys the witch, the witch is absorbed by the tree, the faerie becomes the witch. Around and around on the circle. The Obsidian Revenant always remains. The tree empowers the next faerie. And it continues to grow."

"So, I *am* meant to destroy you?"

"Just as I destroyed the one before me. It is the way it has always been. And now your tithe demands it also."

Perhaps because her fear was abating, Nettle looked at Kole on the floor. The blood had stopped pooling, though the fisher girl remained motionless. "My gifting of Kole…you said it was a mistake. Yet I am now bound to take a life, a life you are openly presenting to me."

"Ah. I said it was the way things have always *been*—" The Erw Witch raised the birds on her hands so they were perched in front of her cavernous eyes. A mirror image of Nettle, of sorts. Two eyes of black, two eyes of white. "—not the way they will continue to go!"

Clenching both fists, the witch released Kole from the grip of the grasping vines, and then sent them after Nettle. Like a many-headed hydra they came for her. She used what energy she had left to defend herself, but these were not disorienting bubbles: a swirling burst of blackness came from her hands instead. It passed in an instant, the nebulous wave that carried purple lightning within it like veins beneath its surface, but it had seared the attacking vines enough that they fell limp to the floor.

From behind the white raven, the Erw Witch raised an eyebrow curiously. She snarled a toothless howl and spat onto the floor once again. "Already you begin your change. The faerie becomes the witch. Around and around. But this boasting of power is futile! The fisherman took a piece of the Obsidian Revenant, and it was enough to weaken you so I might finally break the cycle."

"The Obsidian? I was led to believe they gave *you* strength?"

"It is not for you to understand. Not until you become me. But that will not happen." Throwing a hand forward she launched Nettle across the room, into the wall. "And your weakness is even more glaring, after foolishly giving your strength to the human." She flung the faerie through the air again.

Nettle gathered herself together. She wiped some dim, caliginous blood from her mouth, and caught her own breath before asking, "Were you never tempted yourself? To gift one, too?"

The Erw Witch paused momentarily; the ravens' heads tilted at peculiar angles as well. Perhaps trying to recall all of her experiences in this world.

Nettle pressed. "What did *you* find when you woke here?"

"Only what I was meant to find. I was her before me. She herself was, too." But beneath the witch's riddles, there *was* something else which appeared in her mind; Nettle could sense it. Nettle knew it was there, like a bruise on an apple; the slightly discolored circle under its skin. Though the Erw Witch would not let it vex her. "And nothing else matters."

The witch brought forth the fire once more, directing its fury towards Nettle. Behind her, the wall erupted in flame and her instinct was to unfold her wings and fly out of danger, but nothing happened. Her wings were simply no longer hers. She shielded herself with her arms as the side of the shack came crashing down around her.

Nettle could feel a different power of sorts inside her, however. It was less of a collection of voices teeming with life, and more of a single dark calling in her mind. Holding onto the small table upon which the cloth pouches were piled, she pulled herself to her feet. She caught sight of the witch through the blaze and she picked up and hurled the table at her, knocking the woman to the floor. Some of the bags fell open, and that same unnatural black substance bubbled and singed the floor. The ravens took flight, escaping out through the hole forming in the wall; the fire burned an opening for the birds to sail off into the night sky.

She spotted Kole, still motionless on the floor. She made a move to take the girl in her arms but was met with the sharp end of the harpoon. The witch had stuck the searing metal into Nettle's side; the intense, burning pain shot through her, hurting everywhere. Nettle looked at her own blood-soaked hands— viscous and muddy red—unsurprised to find her life force had lost its luminous glow entirely. Looming above her, the witch cackled madly. Her face smeared with soot.

"You've overestimated what strength you have left, faerie." She let go of the harpoon and kicked Nettle back to the floor. A wooden beam cracked above them, raining down fiery ash. Soon the house was an enraged inferno. The blaze engulfed nearly everything.

The harpoon still stuck in her side, Nettle rose again to face her attacker. She wiped blood and soot from her own face. "And *you* underestimate *me*. And my need to wake from this dream."

The witch spat blood onto the floor. The hungry fire pounced on it and lapped it up. "You will not wake. We never do!"

"I tire of what has been and what is meant to always be. I have been tasked with paying a tithe. And believe me, it is a life I *will* take."

In one swift motion Nettle pulled the harpoon from herself, feeding more fresh blood to the blaze, and stuck it deep into the Erw Witch. Deep enough to pin her to the wall. The witch hissed at her, her black-hole eyes momentarily flared amber-pink; the final sign of another life once lived. Horribly, her skin bubbled in the searing heat, it blackened and began peeling away from her like a snake shedding its skin. But only to reveal a snake which had already been dead inside.

Nettle quickly scanned the house for Kole and found her wrestling with consciousness, atop some withered vines on the blackened floor. By the time she reached the girl and turned back, the Erw Witch was already nothing more than gray bones hanging from the wall. The skull's eyes as black as they'd ever been.

Kole's own eyes widened and glowed brilliantly, elated to see her savior. "Nettle! Are you—?"

Suddenly a mighty crack filled the air as the roof erupted above them, and flames burst upward into the night. The already-crumbling chimney fell to pieces, raining heavy stones upon what was left of the shack. A massive, billowing cloud of smoke and flame reached as high as it might, and bolts of pure white lightning cracked across the Obsidian-black sky.

One moment the girls felt trapped, caught in the house, the blaze engulfing everything around them. The next, they could see nothing but darkness. What had just been in front of them was now muted by sea smoke. The thick mist peeled itself away from the girls and they realized they were back outside, beneath the shadow of the Obsidian Revenant. The house was not there any longer; now nothing more than a smoldering patch upon the rocky precipice of Erw. Ash circled around the hilltop in a dark dance of destruction, and the cawing of two far away ravens could still be heard reverberating off the clouds. The skeleton of the Erw Witch sat crumpled in the brown grass next to them. Nettle reached her hand out and placed it upon the witch's shoulder blades where the tiny bones of long-forgotten wings had deteriorated to nearly nothing.

The sea smoke—what still remained of it—gathered around the bones, masking them from view. Then it spiralled upwards into a great column before fading away entirely. In the aftermath, the Obsidian Revenant appeared slightly more massive and even blacker than before. It continued to absorb the stars' luminosity, and casted frightening howls out into the realm of Erw.

Below it all, the girls held each other. Neither wanting to be the one to let go first. They kissed, for the last time as the fisher girl and the faerie.

CHAPTER 23

SHE FLUTTERED THROUGH THE WOODS; THE WHITE BARK of the birch trees was shiny and slippery with morning dew. Long, prickly canes of berry bushes stretched past where the trees ended until they thinned out into fields of tall brown grass. Still following the trail towards the sound of the ocean's tide, she rose above impassable thickets to the top of a small hill. From there she could clearly see the remains of the fishing village: a dozen or so dwellings that had been smashed and washed away by the ocean. Seabirds stood amongst scattered bricks and saltwater-soaked wooden frames, greedily consuming their morning catch.

Kole continued to fly down to the shore rather than feel the all-too familiar sand beneath her feet; the magnificent freedom of flitting upon the breeze with glimmering wings was surely something she would not soon tire of. Even her bones felt lighter, not unlike the seabirds which caught the wind and took flight with fish in their bills as she drew near.

The tide was out. Nettle sat on the beach, an unmoving speck upon the vastness of sand. In both hands she held the worn cup carefully, now blackened from the fire.

She almost didn't notice as Kole settled herself in the sand beside her.

"Still nothing," Kole said quietly. She had left earlier that morning to search the surrounding shores and fields and woods for any signs of those who had disappeared from the village. Hoping, perhaps futilely, that the destruction of the Erw Witch and the disappearance of the once-incessant sea smoke might have brought them back. That her family might have returned after all.

Not far away at the fishing boat graveyard, a weathered mast that had stood defiantly since being thrown ashore, cracked and crashed into the rest of the boats' debris.

Nettle spoke bluntly. "You won't find them, Kole." She didn't mean to phrase her words so callously; it was just how they came out. Her eyes remained fixed somewhere out in the distance. Past ocean waves. The last thing to go in Nettle's transformation the night before was the iridescence from her eyes. They no longer shined, and one eye was now completely black while the other was pure white. "But I'll keep looking in your absence."

"Absence? Where am I going?" The iridescence in Kole's own eyes was still burgeoning; a glassy, leafy green chroma was becoming far more prevalent than her dark gray. Her amber-pink glow flared a little, too.

"You need to go to Sceanth. You must dissolve my life vein cocoon."

"How would I—?" Even as she said the words, Kole felt a lump in her throat at the prospect of the two of them separating so soon. "Don't you wish to return to the bluebell fields yourself?"

"My place is here now. I must return to the house at the top of Erw."

"But it burned, did it not? There was nothing left."

Nettle still did not understand exactly how things worked

in Erw; nothing of its convoluted cycles, its legends, or of the ocean itself. But that morning certainly felt calmer and quieter than she had yet known. Even the voices of the land's creatures were no longer in her head. She dismissed the thoughts. "That is of no concern," she said without worry, still gazing out over the water's expanse.

Kole tried briefly but did not know where to begin imagining how she might cross over to another world. All she ever really knew of was mending trawler nets and cleaning boats and preparing meals for fishermen, of grim marshlands and serpent shrines. She tried to form images in her head of just how blue the streams of Sceanth might sparkle, how massive the snow-capped Tower Mountains must be, or just how thunderous the footsteps of glimmer giants might echo through the land. Incredibly, something within her was already feeling a connection to the five-winged voros moths.

"You'll like it there," Nettle encouraged.

Kole took her hand. "I like it here, too. Here with you." Their hands were opposites of what they were just days before: Nettle's were now soft and fleshy, while Kole's had a different kind of roughness to them. Before, her hands were calloused from labour and ocean spray, while now they felt similar to leaves at the end of summer. Her fingertips were even beginning to form needle-like points. She drew flowery lines in the sand with a couple of her free fingers.

Finally, Nettle pulled her eyes from the water and turned to Kole. She was about to speak but Kole cut her off. "Nettle, please don't prattle off any of that *circles and cycles* gibberish right now. It's not going to help."

Nettle smiled. "You're learning fast."

"I just want some more time. I'm not ready to leave you just yet."

"I think we can afford a little more time, Kole." She held the charred goblet out. "Will you help me bring this back to your home? I think your mother would be happy to know it's been returned."

"I think she would." Kole accepted the cup. "We can bury it beneath where our hearth once stood."

They brushed the sand from their legs and walked towards the village remains. Already Kole did not enjoy the feeling of her feet on the earth, and wished to fly again, but stayed by Nettle's side. "May I ask you something silly, Nettle?"

"I am sure whatever it is, it is not as silly as asking permission for it."

"It's just…well. If I'm becoming you, and you are becoming the witch, then who will replace *me*?"

"You were nothing before now. There is no need for another to become what you were."

"That is harsh, Nettle."

"I suppose." Nettle thought hard for the right answer, though she did not know for sure what it might be. Finally she said, "But. Perhaps another traveler will cross over into this land, and they will meet another girl from Erw who will mean everything to her."

"I hope so." Kole released a breath that seemed to have been held for some time.

Nettle believed her answer was the right one. For now, at least. "Choosing one's life vein correctly is no easy task, Kole. But in the end, I chose *this* one. And this was the one that led me to *you*."

"And will I return to Erw? Will I find you again?"

"Perhaps." Nettle went still as she thought about the question more seriously and nodded her head slowly in recognition of the verdict she had settled on. "You will. When all the footsteps you left here have long been lost amongst the beach sand, the trails, and the marshes. When you have followed the voros moths to the one place you were really meant to be. When the alder crown you've been given has long since withered and shriveled, or when you've grown tired of playing tricks on glimmer giants or counting poti roots on river currents. And when the footsteps you've yet to take here again are understood by the sea smoke of the ocean, I can be found amidst a foggy patch on a hidden isle. Or wherever else you need to find me. As your family has ever practiced, there is always a place for hope."

There was a sudden splash in the approaching tide behind them. Then an awesome, beautiful roar. The girls turned in time to see the back of the great beast breach the ocean's surface. The greatest sign of hope they could have received, and the greatest time for it.

Nettle placed a cold hand on Kole's neck, running her fingers along the serpent tattoo. "I think," she said slyly, "I may need to get one of these, too."

They watched the serpent until it disappeared over the horizon. Kole felt a peculiar tingle in her hand—the hand that had just been holding Nettle's—and when she turned back, Nettle had vanished, too. Thick sea smoke, crackling with intermittent sparks of amber-pink, drifted up the beach. It passed over a small sandcastle, slipped between husks of boats in the distant graveyard, and was gone.

Not far out in the ocean, there was a shimmering which stole Kole's attention. In the now-clear night, bright blue sparkles danced just above the water's all-too-still surface. She fluttered over for a closer look. What first appeared to be a bubble, was actually a turtle shell-shaped stone jutting out from the surface. It looked a little like a tiny pupil in the center of a big, sparkling eye.

Kole lightly planted herself on it. She stood tall upon the stone then slowly, carefully, dipped a toe into the water. A delicious, alluring chill shot up through her body. There was a staircase of sorts: more stones leading downward beneath the surface of the ocean. She thought about this. Then she turned back to the beach, but no one was there waiting for her to make a choice.

So Kole took a step, then another. Soon, the water touched her knees, her hips, her belly. She retracted her wings. She lifted her arms, fingers splayed, as though trying to balance herself on a branch. The water tickled her shoulder blades.

And then she disappeared from sight. The water did not stir—not a ripple, not a splash. It remained as lifeless as if the faerie had never been there at all.

SHE DID NOT DREAM ANY LONGER. SHE COULD BARELY remember the dreams she once had. Sometimes though, at the oddest of times, bits of her dreams would return in ways she could not make sense of. A beautiful face. An unknown place. And warm feelings that meant very little. A white tree when all she knew now were black ones. A disheveled man disappearing into the brush who would later talk at length about oceans. A coquettish girl with pointed ears and a lime green glow, who placed a crown upon her head.

Today, she was at her table eating soup brewed from dusty roots, rotten berries, and the contents from a worn bottle with a faded label she could not read, but knew it was called Glory. She slurped the soup loudly enough that seabirds screeched in retaliation from far away. And as she ate, an image formed in her mind. A vision of lying entwined with a girl she knew not; warm breath on her cheek and the girl's fingers coiled in her hair. They were twisted together within a shell of sorts. There was also a brief, flitting memory of swimming as a mermaid, the ocean kelp on the seafloor tickling her stomach as she swam through.

But, for today, that was all she saw in her mind's eye. She smiled—a little uncertain of why—before finishing her soup.

She lived in a shack at the top of a rocky precipice. When she wished to see the world below her, she simply asked the sea smoke to clear. And there it was. An icky, gray-brown land of marshes, mud, and sloughs. Its wildlife was rich, though mostly passive. She sometimes felt as though the land's inhabitants should have been more egregious. More bloodthirsty. Perhaps they just needed a nudge. Even from up high she could make out frogs and snakes below, as well as the shiny trails from slugs and snails, all minding their business on the wet shores, within swaying reeds, and over piles of dead leaves and branches. The ocean's tides, however, would inextricably swirl in malicious ways, chasing boats and whatever else it might capture in its grasp.

When she wished to think of worlds not her own, she would read stories from her book. Its pages were weathered and had grown stiff from salt spray. It was an artifact she uncovered while digging through the debris of a village the ocean had mostly washed away. Her book was full of dark ghost stories and frightening tales of witches and strange creatures. In other lands, it read, there existed faeries, beings who enjoyed slipping between worlds to haunt humans and throw cursed gifts their way. Some would steal babies. They would hunt fishermen and sailors by draining the seas from beneath their boats or by singing songs to lure them to unforeseen deaths. Some could spit lightning. Some were vampiric horrors who kept cauldrons full of blood. Some faeries ate other faeries, devouring the glow from their wings. And still others would reach out to save the humans in their times of need. All of the stories began and ended with some amount of ambiguity, and most of them were bleak and grim. She loved these stories, but she might have itched to read one with a happy ending, if happy endings were something she knew existed.

On this day, she decided she would return to the house in the woods. The place she was born into Erw. She packed nothing before departing and left her home on foot. The sea smoke could have taken her there quickly, but she chose to walk instead. There was no rush, for time was just a little more meaningless now. She barely noticed the days go by anymore.

Along the way, she passed a couple of crestfallen fishermen and a Yarari drunk who had stumbled away from those he knew, oblivious to where he was treading. She took the opportunity to give all of them a good scare. A gift of sorts, stories of their own they would be able to carry with them forever. Tales they might pass along to any who needed to hear them. It was enough for another smile to find its way back to her face. If only for a moment. But what is a moment anyway but more meaningless time?

Eventually she found the house in the wooded marshlands. It had always been there, even when it wasn't. The mossy door was ajar as it ever was, and she stepped through without the least bit of caution. She took her time exploring the dilapidated foyer, straightening picture frames on the walls, and taking in the smell of the room's frayed, mildewed curtains—their crimson color made them appear more like sheets of blood hung from the windows. The details of the house were both familiar and unrecognizable. She stopped in front of two charcoal drawings hung next to each other on the wall, and she inspected them: in one, large shadowy waves made a tiny black boat seem like a speck; in the other, the same furious ocean battered an island. She paused for an extended moment, knowing she'd seen these pictures in another life. They spoke to her now in virulent, bitter words. She merely laughed a little laugh their way before moving along.

She walked upstairs. The floorboards creaked in a soothing manner. Scuttling bugs avoided her footsteps and spider webs seemed to blow out of her way as she passed.

At the end of the long hall was the bedroom. There was no door and the hinges hung freely, waving a little as though the entire house was rocking back and forth. Winds blew against the weather-worn windows. Through thin walls she could make out the whooshing of reeds and tall grass outside. She sensed the ocean too, its tide and its briny stink. For some reason it all felt so much more fearsome from this corner of the house.

She looked under the bed and found nothing but trapped shadows and lost nightmares. How she wished they could be set free, but she was learning that some things do not work as she wished they might. There were certain parts of darkness that fell outside her grasp.

She flattened the stale, moth-eaten sheets carefully with her hands, then stood back and contemplated the bed. There were certain details she couldn't make sense of, like a scent that reminds one of something specific, but the memory will only flutter around the answer, never landing squarely upon it. She sat on the bed, but her body felt weak, so she lay down and closed her eyes.

The sea's smoke formed outside, and it crept into the bedroom through cracks in the window.

It filled the room, and when she at last opened her eyes— maybe with the answer she sought, but maybe not—all there was was gray. It crackled like a thundercloud and hummed like the aftermath of death.

She asked the sea smoke to clear and when it did so— unfolding itself until nothing was left—she found herself back outside in the woods. The house was no longer there, though she knew it remained right in front of her. She seized a handful of wet dirt and spat into her palm. Then she returned the earth from where she took it, and something began sprouting immediately. It was a curly white finger at first, then the plant turned green and drooped slightly as a dozen violet tepals bloomed. She admired the single bluebell for some time before shaking her head and sensing the presence of something else.

The Obsidian Revenant loomed in the darkness of the woods. Its thick black roots had sprawled across the mud and marsh. And it was trying to pry inside her head, but she waved it out of her.

"Away with your evil ways," she said to the tree.

"Where…would I go?" it asked in a plodding sort of way. Shadowy eyes formed within its shadowy skin. "You…cannot rid yourself…of me…like you can the sea smoke."

She almost walked away in that moment, but chose to stay, planting her feet more firmly in the dirt. She said nothing more.

"The sea smoke," the tree repeated. "You use it in ways…it was not meant for."

"The house at the top of Erw is *mine* to dwell in now. And I will use the land's powers however I see fit."

"Are you certain…that the ocean…and the serpent…will allow you to?"

"It is the natural harmony of this land. I will maintain it. The sea smoke has no reason to interfere."

"When the girl comes for you…she will come with *other* intentions. It is foolish to think you might reshape the circle."

"Foolish?" She laughed a little at the word, before finally turning from the Obsidian Revenant. "It is more foolish to not ever try."

ACKNOWLEDGEMENTS

It's funny and a little sad how we often need to cycle through friends in order to find the ones that will really click. Or in the case of writing, it's the search for a good critique partner who will also inspire you to try something outside your comfort zone. This book would not have existed without Natalie Pinter, who helped inspire me–certainly unintentionally–to delve into the fantastical worlds of beguiling fae, their gifts and their tithes, as well as a host of other magical creatures and monsters. I fell in love with exploring these new ideas, eventually shaping them into this portal fantasy involving witches, headless chickens, and life vein cocoons.

Thank you also to my publisher for taking a chance on this strange little book.

To all the indie writers who lift me in a variety of ways, to the book's early readers, and to the many established authors (who will likely never read this acknowledgement) who helped me discover the magic in books.

To my MC's who have come before (Isabelle, Tommy, Cepik, and yes even you, Chester). I'm thrilled to add Nettle to such an eclectic mix.

Many big thanks to anyone who's taken the time to read any of my books or short stories. Readers and reviews are really all that any small author is looking for.

Of course, most thanks and love go to my family, for letting me sit in this office and churn out these mostly ridiculous tales, one after another.

ABOUT THE AUTHOR

R. Tim Morris has previously published four novels (*Molt*, *The Inevitable Fall of Tommy Mueller*, *This Never Happened*, and *To Be Honest*), as well as having edited and published a collection of short stories in 2020 (*More Time: A Brief Anthology of Indie Author Short Fiction*). All five books were published under his own imprint, Empire Stamp. Morris has had other works of short fiction published with Owl Canyon Press, Cardigan Press, and Sans Press. *The Lost Memories of Oceans* is his fifth novel.

He lives in Vancouver, Canada, with his wife and two children.

www.ingramcontent.com/pod-product-compliance
Lightning Source LLC
Chambersburg PA
CBHW031530310726
48971CB00008B/2423